Foreign Bodies

Foreign Bodies

Roger Smythe

Copyright © 2023 Roger Smythe

The moral right of the author has been asserted.

Apart from any fair dealing for the purposes of research or private study, or criticism or review, as permitted under the Copyright, Designs and Patents Act 1988, this publication may only be reproduced, stored or transmitted, in any form or by any means, with the prior permission in writing of the publishers, or in the case of reprographic reproduction in accordance with the terms of licences issued by the Copyright Licensing Agency. Enquiries concerning reproduction outside those terms should be sent to the publishers.

This is a work of fiction. Names, characters, businesses, places, events and incidents are either the products of the author's imagination or used in a fictitious manner. Any resemblance to actual persons, living or dead, or actual events is purely coincidental.

Troubador Publishing Ltd
Unit E2 Airfield Business Park,
Harrison Road, Market Harborough,
Leicestershire. LE16 7UL
Tel: 0116 279 2299
Email: books@troubador.co.uk
Web: www.troubador.co.uk/matador

ISBN 978 1805140 252

British Library Cataloguing in Publication Data.
A catalogue record for this book is available from the British Library.

Printed and bound in Great Britain by 4edge Limited
Typeset in 11pt Garamond Pro by Troubador Publishing Ltd, Leicester, UK

Matador is an imprint of Troubador Publishing Ltd

To Csilla with love

ONE

1935

OUTSIDE JODHPUR

The applause overwhelmed her. She didn't think she'd ever felt so happy, so fulfilled.

The sun beat down on the little stage, open to the elements, and the gaudy backcloth flapped lazily in the balmy wind. The actors on either side of her bowed again, and she bowed with them. She could see the faces of all the people sitting on the front row, alive with the joy of the performance, as the whole audience continued to clap enthusiastically. She wanted this moment to go on forever.

Back in the little tent behind the stage, the actors wiped the melting greasepaint from their faces, each jostling for a share of the solitary patchy mirror, leant up against a trestle table. It was even hotter in here than it had been outside, with no breeze to counteract the trapped warmth.

Jenny liked being with these people, she felt at home here. It was the penultimate day of the tour, and she dreaded having to return to her father's bungalow, on the outskirts of

Delhi. It was only because Rosalind, a friend of the family, was in the company that she'd been allowed to be involved at all – British army officers were very protective of their reputation. She sighed, and in that sigh was contained all the contentedness of the last few months, and all the ennui she knew was shortly to come.

She was one of the last to leave the tent, and when she stepped outside the sun had lost its intensity, and the others were already taking apart the stage. She placed the little case containing her costume and make-up in the back of the cart, and went to gather up the props, which lay where they'd been dropped at the end of the performance. She tidied them away, as she always did, into the basket in which they travelled, realising, as she did so, that she'd only pack them away one more time. A tray, a tea set, a feather boa, a pretend pistol, two wads of fake rupees and all the rest of them: a curious, incongruous collection of objects, and yet she handled each with a kind of reverence, a devotion intrinsically undeserved, but bestowed in her mind by an association with the play, with the company, with the world she worshipped.

The two carts trundled off, laden with their theatrical cargo, human and otherwise, and the horses groaned under the strain, but they were used to it. At the next village, the men tethered the horses under a tree and fed them, while the women set about preparing the evening meal, which they all shared under the reddening sky. These were convivial times, and, if she was lucky, Jenny would be passed a swig or two of the local liquor, before the others finished it, and before they all retired to their makeshift beds.

Another day, another performance – the last one.

"I did it because I had to!" Jenny exclaimed, the pretend pistol in her hand, as the audience gasped. "And now, you may do with me what you like."

More applause, more happiness, and then everything packed away for the last time.

1936

Delhi

The little boy ran round her.

"I'm a train, I'm a train!" he shouted.

"No you're not," Jenny laughed. "You're a bird, flying around a mountain, waiting to swoop down on your prey."

The boy made loud squawking noises, and then threw himself onto the floor of the veranda, squirming on all fours and pretending to gobble up whatever it was he'd caught.

"What is it?" Jenny asked.

"It's a mouse," the boy replied.

"Well done!" she congratulated him. "Was it nice?"

"Delicious!" said the boy, pretending to lick his lips. He shook his shock of red hair, and beamed at her. "You play the best games, Jenny."

"Do I?"

"Oh, yes! You're never boring, like my other babysitters. You're always fun."

"Well, thank you! I aim to please."

"Are you very old?"

"I beg your pardon!" Jenny pretended to look shocked. "I'm not old at all. I'm young … very young."

"But you're a grown-up."

"Only just. I'm nearer your age than I am my own father's."

"But how old are you?"

"I'm twenty-one."

"Twenty-one? That's really old!"

"You little scamp!" Jenny ruffled his hair and he smiled again. "Come on, let's go and ask Nisha if there's any cake."

"Rather!"

He ran ahead of her through the French windows and on into the kitchen, and she followed him lazily.

The boy's parents weren't late getting home.

"That was the dullest regimental dinner I've ever had the pleasure of attending." Imogen Styles threw her silk wrap down onto the chaise-longue.

"I'm sorry, my dear, but needs must." Her husband looked rather fine in his full dress uniform. "Have to keep up appearances, you know."

"How was Jackie?" Imogen asked. "Was he good? Did he behave?"

"Good as gold," said Jenny, uncurling herself from an armchair.

"And Nisha?"

"Nisha is lovely, Mrs Styles."

"Oh, she's nice enough to talk to, but she doesn't know the meaning of hard work."

"She helped me get Jackie ready for bed."

"So she should. What time did he go?"

"About eight."

"He should be in bed by seven. When you come again, make sure he is."

"Yes, Mrs Styles." Jenny picked up the script she'd been reading, and her cardigan.

"I'll see you home," said Major Styles.

"Oh, there's no need, sir," said Jenny. "It's only a couple of minutes away."

"Nevertheless," the major insisted.

"Thank you, sir."

As they went along, Jenny thought how silly it was that Major Styles should worry about her walking the short distance to her father's bungalow. Last year, touring with the play, and in the second tour that followed shortly afterwards, she had pretty much been left to her own devices. Rosalind had allowed her a very free rein.

He wished her goodnight at the gate, but waited until she had gone inside and closed the door behind her. She went straight to her room, changed into her nightdress, climbed into bed and finished reading the script.

1937

Delhi

"Jenny! There's a letter for you." Her father called out to her at the bottom of the garden. He was casually dressed, not in uniform; today was a day off. He waved the envelope lazily at her by way of explanation.

"Does it look important?" she called back.

"I don't know. I'll leave it on the table. Your mother and I are going out."

"All right. Thank you."

She sat for a few moments after her father had disappeared back into the bungalow, but curiosity got the better of her. A letter could mean another play, another tour; escape from this daily round of getting up, eating, sitting, occasionally babysitting or going out with her parents, going to bed again. She rocked herself out of her sunny daydream in the deckchair, and crossed the closely cropped lawn. As promised, the letter her father had waved at her was lying on the veranda table, address-side up. It was typed, and she sensed at once that it contained something important. Opening it carefully, she slid out the crisp, single sheet, unfolded it and read. Her heart missed a beat, and she exhaled, slowly.

"They want me to do a screen-test," she told her parents, when they returned later that afternoon. She had spent the intervening hours in a state of high excitement, unable to settle to anything, first lying on her bed, then back at the bottom of the garden, then chatting inconsequentially with Vilina in the kitchen, then tidying her already-tidy wardrobe.

"What's a screen-test?" her mother asked.

"It's where they film you from all angles, and doing a little bit of script – I'll have to learn that – to see if you're any good for the film they're going to make." Jenny knew all about it from the Hollywood magazines she occasionally read, whenever she could get hold of them.

"Heavens!" said her mother.

"It's a sort of audition, really," Jenny explained.

"What's the film?" her father asked.

"It's called 'Gone with the Wind', apparently."

"Gone with the Wind?"

"It's based on a new novel, by an American woman."

"And what's it about?" Major Pearson persisted.

"I'm not sure. I think it's about a young woman, growing up in America, in the Civil War. I've read about it somewhere. Can we go into town now, and see if we can buy it?"

"How do they know about you? Your address – where to write?"

"The letter says one of their talent scouts saw me last year, in 'Lotty's Dilemma', and Auntie Rosemary passed on my address to them. You don't mind, do you? I must do it."

"When is this screen-test?"

"Next week, in Bombay."

"Bombay!" Mrs Pearson exclaimed. "But how will you get there?"

"By train, of course."

"But it'll take you days."

"The screen-test isn't until the end of the week, Friday. There's plenty of time to get there."

"Oh, Jennifer!"

"Please!"

"Of course you must go," her father said, decisively, and his daughter hugged him, before he added, "your mother will go with you."

"Oh, but, father…"

"Gerald!" Mrs Pearson complained. "We've got the Andersons next Wednesday."

"Never mind the Andersons, I'm sure they'll get on very well without us."

"It'll look bad."

"It'll look fine."

"But, well, if they like you," Mrs Pearson continued, turning back to her daughter, "where would you have to go to make this film?"

"I don't know. America, I suppose."

"America! Oh, now, really, Jennifer—"

"No," said Major Pearson. "The decision's made. Write at once and tell them you can go."

"Oh, Gerald!"

"This is a tremendous opportunity for her, Agatha. If Jenny didn't go, it's something she might regret for the rest of her life."

Bombay, Delhi

The audition/screen-test went very well with the camera Rolling and Jenny playing the feisty heroine. They took pictures from all angles and Jenny got the chance to voice the famous lines, "After all tomorrow is another day!"

She was there for what seemed hours and later the talent scout went over to her.

"You are very good Jenny and if it was up to me, I'd cast you like a shot, but I've got to send all the screen-tests over to America and you should know in a few weeks whether the director wants you to go there for further tests.

Jenny moved backwards as the talent scout who said "call me Sam" moved ever closer to her. His breath smelled of tobacco and she was feeling faint as he leered toward her. He squeezed her arm and whispered: "Here's my card, look me up if you come to the US. You are a gorgeous girl and I'm sure I can get you lots of work."

Reeling from this approach, her head spinning, Jenny gasped: "Thanks," and taking his card, she staggered out to her waiting mother.

"Darling," her mother folded her in her arms.

"You look so pale... how did it go?" Jenny told her all

about it and finished with, "I should hear something at the end of the month."

"Darling, I'm so glad, we'll keep our fingers crossed for you!"

Jenny moped around for days, her mind going round thinking about the advances of the talent scout Sam. She didn't dare tell her parents as she knew exactly what would happen; her dream of stardom would be shattered. In the event, she needn't have worried. A letter arrived four weeks later asking her to travel to the US for further tests. She was elated and rushed to her parents telling them all about it.

The director wanted her to go there in 6 months' time and gave a date and time. Her parents were aghast. "Oh gosh Jenny, this is a huge undertaking. How long will you be away? You can't go on your own. John tell her."

Even Major Pearson, who was normally very positive, was shocked.

"Well err… let's think about it… there's no hurry is there?"

There was a silence, a sense of foreboding. Even Jenny was shocked into a thoughtful, sombre mood. She could sense there was a crossroad; an important point in her life. She could fully understand her parents and truth be told, if Sam, the talent scout, was an example of the sort of people she'd have to put up with, she was not sure she'd want this at all… or would she?

After a few months mulling it over Jenny had gone for a walk through the bazaar or market… She was in a daydream, not noticing her surroundings. Thinking only of her dilemma in going to America. She had been unaware of a large gathering of angry Indians who were being whipped into a frenzy by a wild-eyed man who appeared to be dressed like Nehru, with a peaked cap, tunic and dhoti. He was giving a political speech about Independence. Fascinated, Jenny stopped to listen. She had led a protected life in as much as her parents never mentioned politics. The speaker was extremely agitated and screaming at the crowd to get rid of the British. "Quit India" was the prevailing message.

Suddenly, Jenny began to feel very unsafe, she looked round and could see Indian faces turning to look at her. She started to panic and as the men surrounded her jabbering and pointing fingers at her a lone British man in his twenties pushed his way through the crowd ordering them (in reasonable Hindi) to move out of the way. He took her by the arm and whispered anxiously, "Come with me slowly. Why on earth are you here on your own?"

"I didn't realise it was a political meeting." she gasped.

"Never mind that now. Let's get out of here!" He led her slowly away intermittently shouting to the crowd to clear their path.

After they got out of the crowd, Jenny felt her legs go to jelly and she swooned. The young man, whose name she later discovered was Simon, caught her before she fell and carried her to a nearby cafe which was serving lassi (a yoghurt type drink) and chapatis with various food; street food was the UK equivalent. Simon bought her a small amount with a drink and said, "Here drink this and have some food, you're probably hungry."

Jenny was quite weak and the food did seem to revive her. She looked up to see who her benefactor was. He was peering down at her with a concerned look. She was struck with his good looks and attentive manner.

She found out he was local and in the police who, luckily, had been off duty and passing by.

"You must let me take you home, you've had quite a shock!"

She didn't argue and let herself be led by the arm to her parents' bungalow.

Her parents were very relieved and thanked Simon profusely. They invited him to dinner and, even though he protested, Jenny and her parents insisted.

"You must let us thank you somehow."

"Yes, it's getting very dangerous with this 'Quit India' movement."

Major Pearson pushed the boat out and had his cook serve up a roast lamb dinner with all the trimmings. They had an expensive wine and a dessert of trifle. "You must have missed proper British food Simon; it's hard to get a good cook here."

"Oh, you shouldn't have gone to all this trouble sir!" said Simon.

"In any case, I'm used to curries as I've been brought up here – my family came over in the 1850s originating from Scotland."

"Oh," said Mrs Pearson, hurriedly saying that Major Pearson was born in Bristol of Scottish descent.

"What a coincidence!" She said she was of English descent and that they were going back to the UK if this "Quit India" movement became any more threatening.

Simon, however was not on the side of the Raj and held forth at length about the way the Indians were treated. Jenny had not heard anyone speak quite so passionately about India and Independence. She was completely transfixed, not least because he was so handsome. How could a British person speak so eloquently on behalf of the Indians?

Needless to say, Jenny's parents were not in agreement. After Simon had left, thanking them for a splendid dinner and whispering to Jenny he'd see her again, Mrs Pearson was up in arms.

"How could that boy talk in favour of the Indians? He must be left wing, a commie or something. What do you think darling?"

Major Pearson spluttered, "Well he is young my dear. It's all this newfangled way of thinking that blighter Gandhi is spreading. I've no time for it."

"But Father," said Jenny, "it's only his opinion. Besides, I've never heard the other side of the argument… It's fascinating… he's very good looking… don't you think?"

"Poppy cock!" said the major now on his high horse. "The British have done more for the Indians than anyone else. Now they're stabbing us in the back and trying to get rid of us. As for good looking… Pah?"

Jenny knew it was pointless to reason with her father at this time. She continued to listen throughout the remainder of the evening with a very small smile on her face. Simon had certainly caused a stir. He'd made a big impact on her whatever else. She said her goodnights to her parents and went upstairs to lie on her bed dreaming of the dashing Simon.

That weekend he contrived to bump into her and asked her out. She was shocked as she thought she'd never see him again. Their's what you could call a whirlwind romance. They went everywhere together and quickly became inseparable. Her parents didn't approve of course.

"He's too left wing for me," said her father. "He's a nice enough boy, but he's like a damned commie."

"Oh Father," said Jenny, "don't be like that… he's lovely!"

"But have you met his family? They may all be damned native sympathisers!"

"Oh Father!"

"Look, let's go to Simla for the summer it's much cooler up there and you can meet some nice decent boys at the club."

"Oh Father, I don't want to meet anyone else… Simon is the one I like."

"Oh for God's sake… tell her darling," said the major. "Talk some sense into her!"

But Jenny's mother knew better. What she did say however, was she hoped an ace card.

"But Jenny, what about your trip to America and the audition… it's your big chance!"

Jenny was taken aback but after a pause she said: "I'm still thinking about that, but I'm having too much fun with Simon at the moment." Then after another pause she said: "Look Father, you and Mum go to Simla, I'll be alright here… I can look after myself."

Jenny's mother knew she'd never go to America… the writing was on the wall.

And so Jenny never went to America, after a short engagement, she married Simon and settled down in a bungalow not far from hers and Simon's family.

Major Pearson wanted to buy the bungalow as a wedding present, but Simon would have none of it.

"I'll buy one later when we've saved up… this one I'm renting. I may be only a police sergeant, but we'll manage and I'm hoping to be promoted soon."

The Pearsons gave up. "If you can't beat them, join them," said the major.

"Oh, but darling, she's my little girl… will he be able to keep her in the style she's accustomed to?"

"We'll help out when we can."

Jenny and Simon were blissfully happy and it seemed as if they were the golden couple. They were invited to all the big events in the social calendar that the British contingent threw occasionally. Simon wasn't keen on the snobbish military families and drew the line at going up to Simla and the patriotic club.

The children came in quick succession, four in all, one boy and three girls. For those few years they were blissfully happy and Jenny, who was so passionate about the theatre, was swept along on a roller coaster of domestic euphoria. She forgot all about the theatre and her audition in America.

Jenny was in love and everything seemed perfect.

Perfect, but then the fateful day came and, after that, nothing was ever the same.

The fairy tale had ended. It was February, that awful BLACK FEBRUARY.

One of Simon's family had come to see him and he'd just got home from work and was having a bath.

"He won't be long," Jenny said.

She discovered that he was required to talk one of his sisters into returning home. She had moved in with her boyfriend, the leader of the "Quit India" movement in the province. Jenny thought it was her own business, she was over twenty-one and told Simon as much.

"You should mind your own business," she said and, of course that did it!

"You' ve made me look henpecked," he said, storming out of the room, and so he agreed to go, just to prove he was under no one's thumb.

"Do what you want," Jenny snapped, "I don't care!" thus breaking one of her own rules. Never to row when he was going out.

He was silent, then went over to Jenny.

"I'll have my dinner when I return." Then he said, "Cheer up Jen, I'm only going to have a talk." Then he smiled and put his arm round her. "You should see your face. Anyone would think your husband was going to be murdered.

"But Simon he's the leader of the 'Quit India' movement. Don't you realize how much they hate the British?"

"Oh Jen," he said, "you worry too much. I'll be back before you know it. Besides, I'm in the police. I was trained to deal with such things."

With that, he went out and Jenny was left with an awful sense of foreboding.

An hour later, a rickshaw arrived bearing Simon. He had been attacked by fanatical "Quit India" natives spurred on by their leader.

He was very badly hurt with head wounds. They took him to hospital, but he died a few weeks later.

What followed is very painful but, to keep it brief, police arrested some men who were put on trial. Two were convicted of murder and got life. The rest were given custodial sentences.

The two older children were in primary school at the time, but they don't remember much due to the trauma. However, children can forget but Jenny never did. After the funeral, Jenny's parents told her to go to England with the children as she'd be better off there. They were returning to the UK, but had to settle a few things beforehand.

Jenny got a big payout from the insurance company and her father gave her a substantial amount in stocks and shares that would give her an income from dividends for life.

Simon's family left too, some going to Australia, the rest to the UK.

Jenny's parents returned to the UK, but the damp weather proved too much after all the sunshine, and first the major passed away, with pneumonia. Then some years later, her mother got dementia and went into a home. She lasted many years and is buried near Bath.

Jenny and her four children came over on a ship. It took three weeks passing through the Suez Canal, through the Med and past the Bay of Biscay.

And so she left India behind and never returned. Jenny never recovered from the trauma she had suffered. She never talked about her life in India or the death of Simon. It was as if she wanted to block it out of her mind. It was a blank and it was as if it never existed. The two older children knew only of England and, as far as they were concerned, they were British citizens.

Robert couldn't remember anything except vague recollections of his father. The older girl remembered in greater detail and could recollect things. But then girls seem to remember much more than boys.

The two younger girls knew only England.

Jenny would have needed counselling for her traumatic grief, but then there was nothing like that in India at the time.

TWO

1956

BUDAPEST

A Soviet tank trundled menacingly down the narrow thoroughfare. The air was filled with furious shouts, and sporadic bursts of gunfire echoed on either side from the streets that joined it. A ramshackle phalanx of shabbily dressed students was approaching the tank from the far end of the thoroughfare, armed with bricks and home-made fire bombs. Their chant was angry, defiant, an aggressive paean in support of the recently formed liberal government, and a violent rejection of this bellicose foreign attempt to overthrow it.

They advanced faster than the tank, and when they were within twenty metres or so started hurling their bricks, and lighting their Molotov cocktails. The bricks bounced inoffensively off the shell of the tank, or shattered on the cobbles in front of it, only to be crushed by the tank's inevitable progress. The cocktails, when thrown, exploded harmlessly in mid-air, a spectacular, if pointless, firework display. The students continued to make intermittent dashes at the tank, retreating between each, their onslaughts now a desperate shout of defiance, devoid of any genuine hope of victory.

At last the tank fired, a single shot that caught one student full in the chest, dead on impact, and glanced off another, who fell to the ground, screaming. The rest of them ran, scurrying into alleys and side streets, and within seconds the thoroughfare was empty, apart from the trundling tank, which moved on and away to a different battle, and the body of the dead student, and the writhing body of the one who was screaming.

An old, battered truck sped out of a side street and pulled up beside the injured student. Two young men leapt out, one from beside the driver and another from under the rear canvas. As gently as they could, they lifted the still-crying student into the back of the improvised ambulance. One young man sat with the student, and tried to make him as comfortable as he could, while the other climbed in once more beside the driver. Tamás Kanizsa, a dapper, handsome man in his thirties, ground the stick into first gear, and the truck screeched off towards such medical help as these victims of the Soviet invasion could muster.

The body of the dead student lay in the street, unmoved.

1957

LONDON

Trestle tables, placed end-to-end, lined either side of the gloomy church hall. On the left they were covered with tidy, sorted piles of second-hand clothes, faded trousers, skirts, shirts, ties, blouses, knitted jumpers; on the right were clusters of brightly coloured tins of food, evaporated milk, packets of breakfast cereal, sugar, tea. Everything had been donated by well-wishers.

A straggle of tired, uncertain-looking men and women shuffled down the middle of the hall between the clothes and the food, waiting for their turn at the table at the end, which was side on to the others and just in front of the small, green-curtained stage. A bespectacled middle-aged woman sat behind it, pen in hand, stern-faced and unwelcoming, while a younger woman, altogether more sympathetic in appearance, stood to the fore of a little gaggle of other women, a little to one side.

"Next," called the middle-aged woman, officiously. "Name?" she demanded, when the two men at the front of the queue had stepped forward.

"Tamás Kanizsa," the taller of them replied, his voice low, and rich. "And this is my friend, András Lovász."

"Can he not speak for himself?" the woman asked abruptly, adding both names to the list on the sheet of paper in front of her.

"Yes, I can speak," said András, his voice higher and less authoritative.

"He speaks!" intoned Tamás, a twinkle in his eye.

"Your age?" She looked at Tamás.

"Thirty-six, my dear."

She ignored the intimacy. "And you?" she continued, turning to András.

"Twenty-three."

"Twenty-three?" she queried, sharply. He looked older.

"Yes, indeed!" confirmed Tamás. "He is twenty-three."

"I am."

"We have experienced much, these last few months."

"We have."

"Very well." The woman wrote down their ages, and went on without looking up, "Miss Parkin here will look after you."

The young woman stepped forward. "Please, come with me," she said.

"Thank you, Miss Parkin," said Tamás, smiling at the not unattractive young woman.

"Yes. Thank you," András added.

"Do you need any clothes, before we leave?" she asked, as the woman at the table behind them called, "Next!"

"Thank you, no," said Tamás, "we have some little possessions." He held up a small, battered leather case by way of illustration. András held up his too.

"Would you like to take any food?"

"Do you have any pálinka?" Tamás asked.

"I'm sorry? Pálinka?"

"It is the nectar of the Gods!" he enthused. "It is the very source of life!"

"It is brandy," András explained, "Hungarian brandy."

"Oh," said Miss Parkin, "no, no, I'm afraid we don't."

"A pity," mourned Tamás.

"We have no alcohol. Only food and tea. And some cocoa, too, I think."

"Then lead on, Miss Parkin! We will follow you, wherever you choose to take us."

Outside it was a dullish spring morning. There were very few people about as they walked away from the church hall, in its unfashionable Kensington back street. Miss Parkin walked side by side with Tamás, and András followed a step or so behind.

"We have a room for you," explained Miss Parkin, as they went along.

"You are so kind," said Tamás.

"You won't mind sharing?"

"Sharing?" Tamás stopped in his tracks.

The young woman was flustered. "I'm sorry. We're doing our best… really we are."

"Of course," said András. "We don't mind sharing."

"There are so many of you," she said. "It's such a crisis."

"In Hungary we would be hounded," said András. "Here, you help us. We thank you. We thank you very much."

"I am a photographer!" declared Tamás.

"A photographer! Really!" The young woman was impressed.

"I will set up a studio."

"Goodness!"

"When I have bought myself a camera."

"Yes. Of course. The room is just around the corner. We're nearly there."

She climbed the steps of the once-grand terraced house, now divided into flats and bedsits, and searched in her handbag for a key. The Yale lock was stiff, and needed considerable jiggling to encourage the barrels to line up properly. Eventually inside, the hallway smelt damp as she led them up several flights of stairs to the second floor. A peel-off number eight was stuck to the stained, cream-painted door she unlocked with a second Yale key, and this one yielded more easily. It opened onto a cramped, two-room flat, a living room-cum-kitchenette, and a bedroom.

"There is no bathroom," said Tamás, after he had completed his thirty-second inspection of the premises.

"It's along the landing," said the slightly embarrassed young woman. "You share it with the other flat on this floor."

"Share it?"

"And with the two bedsits on the floor above."

"Bedsits?"

"One-room flats."

"*Oh, istenem!*"

"This is very good," placated András. "Thank you, Miss Parkin."

"Miss Parkin. Miss Parkin." Tamás tried out the name. "No, I do not believe you are called Miss Parkin."

"I can assure you I am," said the young woman, embarrassed.

"*Nem, nem!* It does not suit you." He tried it again. "Miss Parkin. *Nem!* Do you have a Christian name?"

"Tamás!" protested András.

"No. It's all right. I don't mind. My first name is Hazel."

"Ah!" exclaimed Tamás with a flourish of his hands. "That is better, that is much better!"

"Is it?" she asked, not knowing quite what to say.

"Hazel! It is a beautiful name, no?"

"Oh. I don't know."

"*Igen!* Like a beautiful English tree! Don't you agree, András?"

"If you say, Tamás."

"I do say!" declared the handsome Hungarian. "Hazel, you do this all the time? Help the refugees? Poor souls like András and me? It is your job?"

"Oh, no," said Hazel, "it's not a job. I mean, I don't get paid. I do this voluntarily. Because I want to. I admire you all so much. The revolution, I mean. Fighting for freedom. Fighting against oppression. It's such a good cause."

"Is that what we are?" asked Tamás, with a sly glint in his eye. "A good cause?"

"Yes. I mean, no." She blushed. "I mean, I admire you. All of you."

"Thank you," said András. "We admire *you*, for helping us."

"So do you have a job?" the other man interrogated. "Do you earn money?"

"No. I'm a student."

"A student!" Tamás sounded impressed. "A student of what?"

"I paint a little. And I draw. I go to art college."

"Art college! You must be very rich!"

"Oh!" said Hazel, taken aback. "Must I?"

"To have no job. And to be an art student. And to help we poor refugees for no money."

"Well, I have a little money, yes."

"Ah!" Tomás purred. "I thought so!"

"It's from my parents," Hazel explained. "They help me out a little."

"You are a lucky girl."

"Hardly a girl," she said, smiling in spite of the protest.

"You are very lucky. Is she not, András?"

"And so are we," said the other man, "to be looked after like this."

"I'll leave you to unpack," Hazel said. "And to get your bearings."

"Unpacking will not take long," said Tamás, dryly. "But where do we find them?"

"Find what?"

"These bearings."

"Oh. No. Sorry. I mean, I'll leave you to find your feet."

"But we know where our feet are! Don't we, András! On the end of our legs."

"I mean," Hazel tried a third time, "I'll leave you to settle in. Give you some time to yourselves."

"Will we see you again, Hazel?" Tamás asked.

"I'll call again later this afternoon, to see how you're getting on. If you'd like me to."

"But we would like you to," said Tamás, dramatically. "We would like that very much."

"Yes, please," said András.

THREE

1958

TROWBRIDGE

Jenny sat at her kitchen table and stroked the red gingham oilcloth that covered it, a sensible choice in case of childhood spillages. She could hear Robert and his two younger sisters playing in the garden. "An argument's on the way," she thought, as Brenda and Wendy interfered more and more with their elder brother's game, but she hadn't the energy to go outside and break it up. Let them sort it out for themselves. Susan was upstairs in her room, playing with her mother's make-up, pretending to be older than her thirteen years.

This wasn't how it was meant to be, a dull August day in England, with the clouds threatening imminent rain; a far cry from the indolent heat of northern India, even more so from the vibrant sunshine of California. She daydreamed herself onto a sunbed in Los Angeles, beside a technicolor blue swimming pool, confidently discussing her next film role with the handsome, high-powered Hollywood producer who lay on the sunbed next to her. If it appealed to her, she would pass it onto her agent, who could sort out the finer details. A thriller, it seemed, with Jenny playing the *femme fatale*, very much in the style of the new *film noir* which was so much in vogue at the moment. If she turned it down, no doubt they'd approach Lauren Bacall. But she liked the sound of it; she'd all but decided to say "yes".

"Mum! Mum!" The anticipated cry came from the garden and broke her dream abruptly. "Mum!" the ten-year-old called again, his voice growing more and more anguished. "Stop them – they're ruining it!"

Jenny heaved herself up from her chair, pushing down on the tabletop to boost her aching legs. What had happened to her? Where was that fine, slim, strong body of twenty years ago? Well, there was her answer: twenty years, the beginning of a marriage, four children, a marriage abruptly cut short, a journey to the other side of the world, a completely different life…

"Mum!"

"I'm coming!" Her irritation boiled over. "For goodness' sake, can't you sort it out yourselves?"

The first spots of rain were beginning to spatter as she stepped down the back step and into the garden. Robert was trying to retrieve his toy war plane from Brenda, who threw it to Wendy, who threw it back again to Brenda.

"Mum!"

"Give the plane back to Robert," Jenny said, wearily.

Brenda hesitated.

"Give it to him!" her mother commanded loudly.

Brenda pushed the plane at Robert with a cheeky smirk. "Here you are, Robbie-baby," she said. "Carry on with your little game."

"You'll all have to come in now, anyway, or you'll get wet through."

"Mum!" Robert whined again.

"I can't help the rain, can I! You can carry on playing inside."

The two girls ran in through the back door, giggling. Robert followed them sulkily. Jenny enjoyed a brief moment of the thickening rain on her face, trying to wash away her depression, before she too went back inside.

Robert was sitting at the kitchen table, knocking the war plane grumpily from one hand to the other. The two girls were nowhere to be seen, up to mischief somewhere else in the house.

"Would you like some squash?" Jenny asked Robert.

"No."

" 'No' what?"

"Thank you."

"That's better."

"I think I'll have a cup of tea." She moved to put the kettle on the gas.

"Can I have a cup of tea?"

"You don't like tea."

"Yes, I do."

"When have you ever had tea?"

"Sometime."

"You haven't had tea."

"I have!"

Jenny gave up the fight.

"Oh, all right, then," she said, and reached down the scuffed metal tea caddy from the shelf.

The kettle boiled and she poured a splash of water into

the teapot, swirling it around to warm it, before emptying the splash away into the stained porcelain sink. She spooned in three sparing teaspoons from the caddy and added the boiling water to about halfway up.

"Does sir take milk in his tea?" she asked.

"What?"

"Do you want milk in your tea?" she repeated.

"Of course I do," said the sullen boy.

"In India you wouldn't."

"What?"

"Not always. Sometimes you'd drink it black, and not too strong, to refresh yourself in the afternoon sun."

"I'm not in India, am I!"

Jenny sighed. "No, you're not," she said. "I suppose you want sugar?"

"Ye-es!" the boy drawled rudely, as if this was obvious.

She stirred the pot, put milk and sugar in the cups and poured out the tea.

"Here you are, sir." She placed the cup and saucer in front of him and sat down at the table with hers. "Leave it a few moments before you drink, or it'll be too hot."

"I know!"

They both sat silently for a minute or two.

"Do something wonderful with your life, Robert."

"Something wonderful?" the boy queried suspiciously.

"Something exciting. Something that makes a mark."

"I was doing something exciting with my plane, till Brenda and Wendy spoiled it!"

"I don't mean that! I mean when you're grown up. Don't just settle for a normal life, don't just take a job, fall in love, get married, have children—"

"I don't want to get married."

"Quite right!"

"I hate girls."

"So do I, sometimes."

Robert took a sip of the tea, and couldn't hide his dislike of it.

"You don't like it."

"It's all right."

"Of course you don't like it. You've never had it before."

"Have!" persisted Robert.

"Okay, *'have!',*" mimicked Jenny back, good-naturedly. She drank her tea. "One day," she went on, "you could be a great actor."

"Could I?" asked the boy.

"Of course you could! *I* could've been a great actress. I *was* a great actress! I murdered people—"

"Really?"

"I made the audience jump, I made them gasp."

"Really murdered someone? Who?"

"Not really, of course. But as an actor you can do anything, pretend anything! You could really fly that plane, you could be a Spitfire pilot in the Battle of Britain!"

"Yeah!" The boy's eyes sparkled excitedly.

"That's what I mean by doing something exciting with your life, Robert. Be an actor! You can do it, I know you can!"

Robert thought about this for a moment or two.

"Would I have to leave home?" he asked eventually.

"Yes! Oh yes!" There was fire in his mother's eyes. "Leave home! Get away from this dull, drab, boring place. Get away from those wretched girls. Make a life for yourself that's better than this. Oh, Robert! Your life must be so much better than this!"

The boy just stared back at her, perplexed by this sudden outpouring. Then he picked up his plane and got down from the table.

"I'm going to play upstairs," he said.

"Aren't you going to finish your tea?" his mother asked.

"Don't like it," he said, and left the room.

"'Don't like it'," Jenny repeated, under her breath, then louder and louder, "don't like it, don't like it, don't like it, don't like it!" until the last was almost a scream.

"Are you all right, Mum?" Robert shouted back from the hall.

"Yes, darling," Jenny called in reply. "I'm fine."

LONDON

The small one-bedroom flat in Kensington had been enlivened: each available surface in both rooms was crammed with little ornaments, cheap china figurines, quaint thatched cottages, pots and vases, plastic London souvenirs, creating a rainbow of gaudy colours. The furniture, though unchanged from when Tamás and András first viewed their new living quarters over a year ago, was decorated with brightly embroidered throws, antimacassars, cushions. The lampshades in the centre of each ceiling had been softened by the addition of translucent tasselled scarves.

Hazel sat on the single armchair provided in the bedroom-cum-kitchenette, while Tamás and András sat, a little apart, on the bed, disguised by its daytime adornment of cushions and embroidery. A half-finished bottle of pálinka stood on the formica kichenette work surface. Hazel played with her hardly-touched glass rather nervously; András took regular, steady sips; Tamás's glass was already empty.

"You will lend me the money?" asked Tamás, without a doubt in his mind that she would answer in the affirmative.

"Of course," said Hazel, fulfilling his every expectation.

"You are an angel," beamed Tamás, raising his empty glass to her.

"No," corrected Hazel. "Not an angel, just an investor."

"An angel is an investor, if you work in the theatre," explained Tamás.

"I see. I didn't know."

"I will pay you back."

"I know."

"I take some photos. They will be very good. I will earn money."

"You'll be a great success. I'm sure of it."

Tamás leapt to his feet and crossed to the kitchenette.

"Let us toast my success," he said, picking up the bottle of pálinka. "Here, Hazel!"

Hazel put her hand over her glass. "No, Tamás."

He pushed her hand away. "Nonsense! Of course you must!"

"If she doesn't want it, she doesn't want it," urged András on Hazel's behalf, but by then the young woman's glass was topped up and his own had been almost refilled too.

"You, too, András," insisted the festive photographer, as he poured.

András gave Hazel a wry smile. "What's the use of arguing with him!" he said.

Hazel returned the smile. "It's fine," she said.

By now, Tamás's own glass was already refilled to the brim.

"To my very great success!" he enthused, raising his glass in a toast.

"To your very great success!" the other two responded, and they all drank: Hazel barely a sip, almost just a sniff, András a sip and Tamás a slug.

"To England!" the elder man persisted.

"To England," Hazel and András repeated, before another sniff, sip and slug.

"To freedom!" was Tamás's last exultation, and he drained his glass.

"Yes – to freedom," repeated András, quietly and sincerely, before he took a deep draught of pálinka.

"To freedom," said Hazel, and she sipped from her glass.

TROWBRIDGE

Robert sat in his small bedroom. Brenda and Wendy were now terrorising their older sister in the girls' larger room, grilling Susan for the latest tips on make-up and fashion. He'd heard his mother's anguished cry from the kitchen, and didn't quite believe her protestation that she was "fine". If anyone was upsetting her, making her unhappy, he'd murder them. And he'd start with his younger sisters; that would kill two birds with one stone, for they upset him too. He'd leave his older sister, though, let her live; she might even help him. His mother wouldn't mind; she'd practically encouraged him to do it.

It would be good to make it a long, slow death, so Brenda and Wendy knew what was happening, knew why he was doing it, that he hated them, hated the way they upset his mother, hated the way they upset him. Poison, perhaps, with no way of stopping it, so they'd be in pain and could stare at him in agony as he laughed at them dying. He could slip it into the milk before they poured it on their Rice Krispies, and then pour the milk away before his mum or Susan got to it; Brenda and Wendy were always first down to the breakfast table in the morning. His mum would just think they were ill, send for the doctor, but it would be too late. She'd be sad, of course, but happier in the long run, he was sure of that.

But where to get hold of the poison? Not an easy thing to do for a boy of ten. But, then again, when you're ten anything is possible, isn't it. He'd have to think about it, work out a plan, like the Secret Seven or the Famous Five. Yes, that's what he'd do.

He picked up the toy plane from his lap and made it fly through the air, humming a buzzy engine noise between his lips, before the buzz turned into machine gun fire, and the little plane dive-bombed a Matchbox lorry that had been left lying on the floor from the previous day's play.

FOUR

1960

LONDON

Although the middle of a sunny afternoon, the electric light blazed away in the main room-cum-kitchenette of the Kensington flat. A sheet, off-white from repeated washings, had been suspended from hooks on the picture rail, and the armchair pushed out of the way of the sheet.

An attractive young woman, dressed in a high-necked yellow shirt and blue trousers, was posing in front of this makeshift backcloth, as Tamás moved around in front of her, taking photographs from different angles with a large-lensed camera.

"This is good, yes? Lovely!" he said encouragingly, as he clicked away. "You will get many jobs from this. Much acting."

The door from the landing opened and András started to come in, a woven shopping bag of groceries in his hand. Tamás turned on him sharply.

"*Nem most!* Not now, András!" he snapped. "I'm working! Shoo! Shoo!"

András sheepishly closed the door and sat down patiently on the landing floor outside, the shopping bag tucked beside him. Inside the flat, Tamás turned back to the girl and started clicking away with the camera again.

"You tell all your friends, yes?" he said. "I do this for free and you tell all your friends. They will pay me. It will be our secret. Why not! It is good!"

* * *

"A thousand apologies, my friend," appeased Tamás. By now they often spoke English even when they were alone together, a habit of their newly adopted country, and good practice. It was Tamás's dream to become an English gentleman, an eccentric English gentleman.

András picked himself up from the landing floor and stepped into the flat, just as they heard, two storeys beneath them, the young actress let herself out of the building with a click of the front door. "You know how it is! Work is work!"

"Did she pay you?"

"She will tell her friends. They will pay me."

"So we still only have my money this week." András worked six nights a week, minding a department store in nearby Knightsridge.

"Pff!" Tamás exclaimed derisively. "Your money will be nothing compared to what I will soon be earning!"

"Still, it is money," András said, practically.

He started to unpack his shopping from the basket.

"Did you get the pálinka?" Tamás asked impatiently.

"The shop downstairs doesn't sell it. I have to walk a long way if I want to get pálinka."

"You didn't get the pálinka?" The panic grew in Tamás's voice.

"Yes, I got the pálinka." András drew a bottle out of the basket.

"Ah! András!" Tamás's eyes twinked. "You are teasing me! You are very bad! I need my pálinka – I need it now!"

"It is only four o'clock, Tamás."

"It is *at least* four o'clock, András!" The would-be photographer snatched up the bottle. "The pálinka is overdue."

He poured a healthy slug into a glass and sat down in the armchair, without moving it from its new, out-of-the-way position.

"Are you not going to join me?" he asked, suddenly realising he was drinking alone.

"It is only four o'clock," the younger man repeated wearily, emptying the remaining tins and vegetables out of the shopping bag.

"Ah, well," conceded the other. "You will suit yourself."

"I will," said András, and he lit a pungent, gassy flame under a kettle of water.

TROWBRIDGE

Uncle Arthur had come to visit. The children were always excited whenever Uncle Arthur came to visit, because every time he came he could be relied upon to bring each child a present. Even Susan, now a sophisticated, mature young woman of fifteen years old, experienced a little butterfly in her stomach at the anticipation of what this month's little gift might be. Robert at twelve was certainly not too old to be impressed by his uncle's offerings, and the younger Wendy and Brenda were beside themselves with excitement when their mother told them Uncle Arthur was coming for tea that day.

Uncle Arthur wasn't a real uncle. He was a friend of the family. It was odd, Jenny thought to herself, how largely friends of the family featured in her life, first Rosalind in India, now Arthur here in Trowbridge.

"You shouldn't," Jenny said to her pretend brother-in-law when they were settled in the sitting room, and the children had taken their booty to their respective rooms.

"What else are uncles for?" Arthur protested. "Besides, I enjoy it. I've no other children to buy presents for."

"That's not the point. You shouldn't."

Arthur didn't answer.

"How are you?" he asked, after a short silence.

"Oh." Jenny hesitated. "You know," she said at length.

"No. I don't. It must be very difficult for you. Four children is quite a handful, and Susan is getting to a tricky age, I'd imagine."

"Oh, Susan's all right! Susan's the least of my problems."

"So what *are* your problems?"

"Oh." A pause. "You know," Jenny repeated.

"Tell me. Please."

"Just being here, I suppose."

"I'm sorry," said her "brother-in-law", looking at the floor.

"No!" Jenny was cross with herself. "I didn't mean that. You've been marvellous. Without you, we'd've been lost, God knows where."

"Trowbridge seemed the sensible choice. Near me,

near us. And you couldn't have stayed in London. Far too cramped a flat."

"I know."

"And you definitely couldn't have stayed in India."

"No." It was a quiet, breathy exhalation, full of regret.

"India wasn't safe. Not for anyone who had anything to do with the British army."

"I know."

"Especially after poor Simon—"

"*I know, Arthur!*" Jenny exclaimed in a burst of sudden anger, in spite of herself. "Oh, my God, I know!"

"Of course you do," he said quietly. "I'm sorry. But you had to think of the children."

Softly again, "I know. I did."

"And then this house came available."

"It's fine." Jenny thought of her parents' bungalow, of days in the sun, of unfulfilled ambitions, of a lost, carefree life, and of her drab, drab, drab existence in Wiltshire. "It's fine," she said.

FIVE

1962

LONDON

The sun was shining as Hazel and Tamás stepped out of the underground station into the dazzling bustle of Oxford Street, and walked the short distance east before turning left into Bond Street. Hazel led the way briskly, crossing Brook Street, before stopping in front of a narrow shopfront on their right, a traditional men's outfitters.

"It's above here," she said.

"Bond Street! It is good, Hazel!" Tamás sounded impressed.

Hazel dug around in her handbag for the keys. "They're in here somewhere," she said.

A mortice key unlocked the windowless door to the right of the shopfront, and this opened immediately onto a cramped staircase, walled in on either side. There were two doors on the first landing, but Hazel led Tamás on up a second flight, and then a third, to the top of the building. A Yale key gave admittance to the door at the back of the landing. It was a single, largish room, completely empty and with bare floorboards, but a sizeable sash window that looked out over the rear of the buildings on Avery Row.

"Do you think it'll do?" asked Hazel anxiously.

"It's perfect!" Tamás beamed. "*Tökéletes!* This window here, it lets in much light. We will only need to buy one lamp."

"It's seven pounds a week."

"Perfect," said Tamás again.

"I've paid the first month in advance."

"That is good."

"And the deposit."

"They will be happy to come here, all the famous actors." Tamás was tired of discussing the financial arrangements. "I will take their pictures. We will hold an exhibition."

"That sounds perfect," said Hazel, repeating the word a third time.

"Thank you, Hazel," said Tamás gratefully. "You have done well. I am so pleased."

"If you're pleased, Tamás, then so am I." She felt a pleasing flush of warmth wash through her.

"We must waste no time," the photographer enthused. "We must put an advert in the *Evening Standard*."

"I'll call them straight away," said Hazel.

* * *

Hazel lived in a bedsit, a single room that served as living room, kitchen and bedroom, and her bathroom and toilet were outside the room, shared with other bedsits on the same landing; nothing like as spacious as Tamás's and András's flat. It also served as her studio, when she was working at home, and not in the shared studio at art college.

Her course was supposed to last three years, but she was already into her fourth, and happy just to carry on without any particular end in view. The college were happy with this loose arrangement, too, so long as she paid her fees, which, again, she was happy to do.

Her main artistic passion was painting, whether with oils, acrylics or watercolours, she really didn't mind, and her style was almost representational, though in bold, broad strokes. Anyone looking at her depiction of Berkely Square in the sunshine, and who didn't know her personally, would assume Hazel to be a forthright woman with strong opinions for which she wasn't afraid to fight. And, indeed, she did have strong and firmly held opinions, but either she kept them to herself, or expressed them so modestly that a casual observer might imagine she couldn't really care less.

Her other main passion, at least for the last three or four years, was Tamás, which grew out of her ardent support for the Hungarian uprising and all other current humanitarian causes. András was very sweet, too, a faithful sidekick to her hero, but rather young and a bit of a drip. In Tamás she saw an enthusiasm for all things artistic, an enthusiasm she shared, of course; she also saw in him a hugely attractive, bewitching man, albeit quite a few years older than herself. In a way, although she didn't acknowledge it in so many words to herself, she loved him. She certainly felt no qualms about helping him in every way she could, both practically and financially, and Tamás, of course, was more than happy to accept her assistance.

If Hazel was honest with herself, which mostly she

wasn't, she'd have done anything for Tamás, absolutely anything he asked of her. Or didn't even ask, if she thought it would benefit him.

TROWBRIDGE

Aidan Harvey kicked a stone down the pavement. He was angry, though there was no way he could articulate at what. His mum was out with a crowd of other women, drinking somewhere; his dad he hadn't seen for the last thirteen of his sixteen years; his brothers, both younger and older, couldn't care less about him; and his friends, well, they'd gone off together somewhere without telling him. He couldn't find them, anyway. Aidan was on his own, and bored.

He picked up another stone and felt its weight in his hand, which pleased him, and his spirits lifted a little. A good thing to throw, he thought. At what? At a window, why not. Whose? It didn't matter, so long as it wasn't his own. In fact, why not his own, so long as it wasn't his actual bedroom. Or, rather, the bedroom he shared with his older brother, Kev. That would show her. She'd have to put up cardboard, or go without drink for a week to pay for new glass. Or he'd have to go without a few meals. Not that that wasn't already a common occurrence. If so, no problem; he'd just nick a couple of Mars bars from Hooper's shop on the corner. Simple.

He looked up and down the street to see no-one was watching him. He checked the nearby windows, as well, but couldn't see any faces, unless they were behind the nets. Satisfied he was safe, he measured the distance in his head, and then hurled the stone with considerable force at their front room window, a force made all the more powerful by his unarticulated anger. The shatter of glass was louder than he'd imagined. He took to his heels, and raced down the street, the opposite way to Hooper's, and round the corner to the little park across the way; well, scrubland with a slide, a swing, a seesaw and a roundabout described it better. Kev was there, sitting on the roundabout, revolving slowly.

"Want a fag?" he asked, as Aidan sauntered up, disguising his rapid escape.

"Go on, then."

Aidan took the cigarette and accepted the match Kev struck for him.

"Was that you?" Kev asked, when Aidan had sucked on his cigarette.

"What?"

"The smash. The glass. Window, was it?"

Aidan looked at his brother.

"Yeah, that's right," he said.

SIX

1966

LONDON

Robert climbed down onto the platform at Paddington Station. It wasn't the first time he'd been to London; of course it wasn't. After all, he'd lived there for a few months, when he was six, when his mother and the girls had first arrived from India, before moving down to the house in Trowbridge. And his mother had brought them all up to town again several times since, to see the sights, and for theatre trips. Only a couple of years ago they'd all come up to the New Theatre, to see the musical "Oliver!". Robert had loved it. What he wouldn't give to play Bill Sykes! But this was the first time he'd been up to London on his own, and he was excited, and scared.

He gave his ticket to the collector at the barrier, and made his way to the escalator for the underground; he remembered where it was from a couple of years ago. He checked his prospective journey on the map on the wall, one change at Euston onto the Northern Line, and bought a ticket to Goodge Street. His mother had given him enough money for all the train journeys, and for something to eat before he travelled back to Trowbridge. The rich red tube train thundered out of the tunnel into the subterranean station and the doors slid open. Robert found a spare seat easily, as it was the middle of the day; he settled down and took out a London A to Z map book from his pocket, just to confirm again his route from Goodge Street Station to his destination: across Tottenham Court Road and along Chenies Street into Gower Street, it should take five or ten minutes at most. He'd been over it again and again with his mother at the kitchen table.

He arrived with twenty minutes to spare and stood on the pavement, looking up at the imposing building front. He took a deep breath, pushed open the door and announced himself as Robert Markham, here for his two o'clock audition for the Royal Academy of Dramatic Art.

* * *

The studio was quite a success, and by word of mouth the clients kept coming; aspirant actors, models, musicians to start with, but then more established names, even one or two knights of stage and screen. Tamás took it all in his stride: he was talented, a genius, of course they came to him for their photographs, why wouldn't they? Hazel was quietly pleased, looking on Tamás as her, albeit older than herself, protégé. She was content with how things were, at least for the time being; she wanted nothing more from him than his friendship and his respect, which she thought she had. She relished the evenings round at his flat, the extravagant, elaborate meals he cooked for her and András, who was still Tamás's room-mate, the ever-flowing wine and palinka, for which she was acquiring, very gradually, a taste.

Tamás was not called Tamás anymore, he was called Thomas, easier for his clients to read and pronounce, and remember, and another step along the path to his becoming an English gentleman. András was still called András, and he still worked as a night security guard at the Knightsbridge department store. As Thomas had predicted, but András had doubted, the photographer's income did indeed now far exceed his younger friend's meagre salary. So the flat was no longer the same flat, but a far more distinguished affair, still in Kensington, but with a bedroom each for Thomas and András, not to mention a spare bedroom for guests, a separate kitchen, its own bathroom, and a living room that was still adorned, like its predecessor, with a cluttered array of ornaments, trinkets and colourful embroidery.

Thomas was holding court, as he often did. "Today my studio was busy from ten o'clock till six o'clock! There was not a spare moment for me to eat, or drink! And how happy they all were, my models! And how they pay! Soon I will be able to afford a larger studio, one that is better suited to the finest photographer in London."

András smiled wryly; he'd heard this speech many times before.

"And if in London, then in England, in Europe!" Thomas continued.

"I think the studio is fine where it is," reasoned Hazel. "Bond Street. You couldn't hope for a better address."

"*Isten!*" exclaimed Thomas. "But it is so small! There is no waiting room. My clients have to sit on a chair on the landing, or at the side of the room while I photograph the person before them. It is not right. It is not appropriate."

"They don't complain, do they?"

"No, but when someone rings the doorbell I must go all the way down three flights of stairs. Three! And then all the way up again, even if I'm in the middle of a session."

"You've not long taken on the expense of this new flat, and that's quite a stretch, isn't it."

"Pff!" Thomas couldn't even find an actual word, English or Hungarian, to express his contempt for this sentiment.

"Much better to see how thing go for a while," persisted Hazel, used to exchanges like this. "Don't go rushing into anything."

"It is good to rush," said the older man. "If you think too much, you get scared. Much better to act on impulse."

"Not always," said Hazel.

"Keep your ears open, Hazel," insisted the photographer. "See if you can find what's available, and for a good price."

"Of course I will, Thomas. But London is very expensive now; it's getting worse all the time."

"Well, you will help me if I need a little extra. Won't you, Hazel?"

"Hazel has her own expenses," protested András. "She can't go on giving money to you all the time."

"Lending money, you mean, András," corrected Thomas. "I will pay her back. Of course I will."

"Will you?"

"Of course he will," said Hazel.

Delhi

The door opened and a smartly dressed man stepped out into the sun. He was not old, not young, in his thirties perhaps. Handsome, in his way, and dressed in a manner that more reflected the old days of the British Raj than modern-day India, white linen suit, brown leather brogues, panama hat.

He stood still for a moment, taking in the busy scene playing out in front of him, the hooting cars, the hand-pulled carts, the bustling pedestrians walking every which way, like a swarm of flying ants worrying the dust of a sidewalk on the hottest day of the year. His hand went involuntarily to his neatly-clipped ginger moustache, and he stroked it idly with his first and second fingers, unthinkingly measuring its length. There was a look of steely determination in his eyes; if you contemplated contradicting him just now, you might think twice about it.

He walked down the two or three steps into the bustling thoroughfare and turned towards the post office, intending to dispatch by airmail the handwritten letter in his pocket. He communicated with the recipient regularly, had done so for many years now. It's good to stay in touch.

But this innocent mission was by way of a diversion from his main purpose today; that lay beyond the post office, beyond the city centre, in a dirty little backstreet on the outskirts. It was a course of action he'd been contemplating for some time now. If something got in your way, it was best to deal with it head on, remove it, so you didn't have to worry about it anymore. At least, that's the way he saw things.

The airmail letter attended to, he made his way by foot

to his primary destination, breaking his journey only once more, to acquire something he needed to bring these matters to a satisfactory conclusion. It was compact, and black, and fitted comfortably into his hand, and easy to get hold of if you knew where to go. And he was sure, once he'd squeezed the trigger, that all his present irritations would be removed.

SEVEN

1969

LONDON

Robert rang the bell on the frame beside the door in Bond Street and waited. He waited for several minutes. He was just about to press the button again, when he heard footsteps coming down a bare wooden staircase behind the door. It opened, and a neat, compact man, with ever-so-slightly thinning hair and a purple cravat, appeared before him.

"Mr Kanizsa?" Robert asked.

"Thomas! Call me Thomas!" the man declared abruptly. "I am busy. You are early. Come, follow, follow!"

Thomas turned his back on Robert and started back up the stairs, leaving the twenty-one-year-old to come inside, close the door behind him and follow on up to the top floor.

"You sit here!" Thomas commanded, indicating two plain, bentwood chairs side by side next to the door at the back of the landing.

"I'm sorry if I'm early," Robert said nervously.

"It's of no matter."

"I don't like to be late."

"It's of no matter," the photographer repeated, and disappeared through the door, shutting it firmly behind him.

Robert hesitated for a moment or two, trying to decide which of the two chairs to sit on, as if it made any difference. He thought about lighting a cigarette, but decided against it, and went to look out of the little window that faced the rear of the building: backs of other buildings opposite him, and a tiny, empty, walled yard three storeys beneath. He turned, chose the chair furthest from the door and settled down.

He'd had his photo taken before, of course, but these were important ones, a particular shot to be chosen, copied, and sent round: to agents, in the hope that they'd take him on as a client; to theatres, television and film producers, in the hope that they'd invite him for an audition, offer him a job.

His three years at drama school had gone so quickly, and now they were nearly over. Had he learned much about acting? A little, he supposed, but he could do that anyway before he went; he'd been quite the star of his school plays, back in Trowbridge. About life he'd learnt a fair bit, looking after himself, sharing a little flat, though that was coming to an end, and the occasional romance, though nothing serious. One more drama school production to go, and he'd been lucky enough to land a good role, the Duke of Cornwall in "King Lear". As his mother had said, you can do anything when you're an actor, even stamp out someone's eyes; it was a showy part, the agents should notice him.

All of a sudden the door burst open, making Robert jump.

"Come and see me again in a week and I will show you the pictures," he could hear Thomas saying inside the room. "You will be delighted, very delighted."

An actor Robert thought he recognised from a play he'd seen on television emerged from the room, said his thank-yous, nodded an acknowledgement to Robert and set off down the stairs. Robert was looking after him, trying to place him, to remember his name, when Thomas barked behind him, "Come in, come in. There's no time to lose. You are not my last model today."

Robert went into the room, much better appointed now than the bare shell Thomas and Hazel had first viewed, seven years ago, with black and white screens to use as backgrounds, and an assortment of lamps to provide various qualities of light.

"Thank you for seeing me," Robert began.

"It is business," said Thomas, curtly. "You saw my card?"

"On the noticeboard, yes."

"You know my terms?"

"I – er – yes."

"You can pay them?"

"Er – yes."

"*Jó.* Good. You want headshots, for an agent?"

"And to send round for jobs."

"But of course. Take off your jacket, please."

"Oh. Do you think—?"

"I think. *Igen.* Take off your jacket."

Robert did as he was told.

"And your jumper."

"Oh—"

"Your – what do you call it? – your cardigan."

"Yes, of course – if you think it best."

"I know what's best. You can trust Thomas. A light background, I think."

"Yes, a light background."

"You are dark, with strong features. A light background will set these off best."

Thomas arranged the background and placed Robert in front of it, then fiddled with the lamps until he got the effect he wanted.

"Is this good?" Robert asked.

"Good? Of course it is good," said Thomas, and he started taking photos, talking all the while. "Look to me, please. That's good. Turn sideways, look down, then up at me." Snap, snap, snap. "Do you live here in London?"

"Yes, of course. I'm at RADA."

"I know you are. You like acting?"

"Well, yes, of course. Otherwise I wouldn't be there."

"It is not always so. Some of your friends, they come to me, and I can see it in their eyes, as I take their photographs, they do not really care about acting."

"Oh, no?"

"Not really care, with a fire in their belly, like I care about taking photographs. You care."

"Oh. Do I?"

"Of course you do, I can see it in your eyes, behind your eyes."

"Oh. Good."

"These photographs will be splendid."

"Good."

"I can sense it. They will get you much work, and you can tell all your friends. 'Go to Thomas!' you can say. 'Go to

Thomas! He will get you work! He will get you jobs, many jobs!'."

"Yes. Yes, I will."

* * *

A week later, Robert was back in the Bond Street studio, looking through a couple of sheets of contact prints, trying to choose his favourite. The two men stood side by side at the window. Thomas had circled three or four of the photos in biro.

"These are the best," he said. "They are all good, of course, but these capture you best, *a lelked*, your inner soul."

"You think so?"

"I think so."

"I need two, they say. A smiley one, and a serious one."

"Then you must choose."

Robert examined the circled pictures again. It was so hard to decide. "This one, I think," he said. "And this one."

"*Kiváló!* I will print these two up for you, ten inches by eight inches, and you can look again. If you don't like them, we will choose again."

"Thank you."

"It will cost more, of course."

"Of course."

"You are busy now?"

"Busy? Oh – er – no, not busy straight away. I have to be in rehearsals at six o'clock this evening."

"Good! I have no more models until 2 pm. You drink?"

"Drink?"

"Yes. It is lunchtime. We can go to have a drink together."

"Oh – yes – of course. That would be very nice."

"The Spread Eagle pub, it is just around the corner. Come."

* * *

The pub was quite busy, it being lunchtime, but Thomas commandeered a table for two in a dark corner, while Robert bought the drinks at the bar, a half pint of bitter for himself, and a large scotch whisky for Thomas.

"*Egészségére!*" said Thomas, as he took his first, healthy sip.

"Do you want anything to eat?" Robert asked. "I think they do pork pies or whatever."

"*Nem! Nem!*" exclaimed Thomas. "The pork pie, it is an abomination! *Fasírozott!* That is what I'd eat! Not all this pastry. Pastry, pastry! You are obsessed with pastry! And whisky, always the whisky!"

"Is the whisky no good? I don't really drink it myself."

"If there is no pálinka, then the whisky is fine. I have asked the landlord a dozen times, more, but he will not keep it. 'I cannot buy it just for you,' he says. 'Why not?' I say, but what can you do!"

Robert didn't know how to answer this, so said nothing, and they sat in silence for a few moments. Thomas seemed lost in his own thoughts. He took another glug from his glass and pulled a face, as if to demonstrate his continuing irritation that it was whisky and not pálinka.

"You live in London?" he asked Robert eventually.

"Yes, in Tooting."

"Tooting," Thomas repeated thoughtfully, trying out the word as if it held a special significance. "Tooting."

"Yes."

"Tooting Bec and Tooting Broadway."

"That's right."

"I read them on the Metro map."

"Metro?"

"Underground map! Pff! In Budapest we have the Metro."

"Ah."

"I have never been to Tooting Bec or Tooting Broadway."

"No?"

"Which station do you go to?"

"Er – Tooting Bec."

"What is it, this 'Bec'?"

"Oh. I don't really know. A beck is a stream, I think."

"A stream?"

"Yes. You know, a little river. But that has a 'k' on the end, so I'm not sure."

Thomas had another slug of whisky, emptying his glass, and Robert took another sip of his beer. "You live in a flat?"

"A bedsit, yes. But my lease runs out soon, just after I finish my course, and the landlord has already let it to another student for next term, so I'll have to find somewhere else. Perhaps I'll go home to Trowbridge."

"Trowbridge. Where is this?"

"It's a town. In Wiltshire."

"This is in the country?"

"Yes."

"But you are an actor. You must live in London."

"Well, yes, but London is so expensive."

"Come and live with me!"

"Oh!"

"I have a spare room, you can stay there. I will charge you very little money."

"Well – thank you. But – well – where do you live?"

"I have a flat, in Kensington."

"Oh, that's perfect."

"Of course."

"Do you live on your own?"

"*Nem, nem!* Another man lives with me also."

"Oh! I wouldn't want to be in the way."

"You wouldn't be in the way. What do you mean, 'in the way'?"

"Well…" Robert trailed off.

"His name is András. We came to England together, after the *forradalom*, the revolution. We are *bajtársak*, comrades."

"Oh, I see."

"Good! It is decided."

"Well, yes, but – I mean, are you sure?"

"Of course I'm sure. When your lease runs out, you will come and live with me."

"Thank you."

"When is your next free evening?"

"Oh – er – Saturday, I think."

"You will come to dinner. You can see the room." Thomas held up his glass. "So," he demanded, "another whisky," – he pulled a face at the thought of it – "to seal the deal."

"Yes, of course." Robert stood up and took Thomas's glass, secretly calculating how much cash he had left in his pocket.

Trowbridge

Susan had hoped that the sun would be shining, but the

clouds resolutely refused to blow over. Her dress was elaborate, more elaborate than she would've liked herself, but her mother had insisted. "It's your special day, darling," she had said. "You must make an effort." Susan thought she *was* making an effort, but rather than have an argument she chose the easiest course. There'd been enough arguments over the last few months, in the build-up to the wedding. She was very much in love with Peter, the local GP she'd met only two years ago: they had the rest of their lives before them; a dress would make very little difference to any of that.

If Susan was dissatisfied with the dress she was wearing, then that was nothing compared to the seething hatred Brenda felt for the flouncy bridesmaid confection her mother had made her sixteen-year-old daughter wear. Duty grudgingly done, Brenda stomped out of the florally bestrewn function room, where the reception speeches had just finished: "actor" brother Robert and "Uncle" Arthur one each, in lieu of Susan's long-departed father, Peter, and finally Peter's best man, an old friend from medical school who was not quite as amusing as he himself thought he was. Brenda plonked herself down on the wall beside the pavement. She noticed a smudge of dirt on the skirt. Good!

A car came speeding up from the traffic lights, and as it passed her, she noticed a young man leaning against a shop window on the other side of the road. He was watching her, and she insolently returned his gaze. He smiled and lazily set off across the road to join her.

"All right?" he asked.

"What's it to you?"

"Nothing."

"I like the dress."

"Fuck off."

"Watch it."

"Why should I?"

He sat down beside her.

"Want a fag?"

Without a word, she took one from the crumpled packet that Aidan Harvey, three years Brenda's senior, offered, and his hand brushed against hers as he held up a struck match to light it for her. She didn't object.

"Are you watching me?" she asked.

"No."

"Haven't seen you for a while."

"Haven't seen *you*."

"Well, you're seeing me now, aren't you."

Aidan lit himself a cigarette, and they sat in silence for a while, smoking.

"Want to go to the Red Lion later tonight?" he ventured at last.

"Are you asking?"

"Sounds like it."

"Might do."

"I'm meeting this bloke. Might get some pot."

"Oh yeah?"

More smoking.

"So, are you coming then?"

"All right."

"Smart."

"I'll have to dodge my mum."

"You can do that."

He slid off the wall.

"See you later, then."
"Yeah."
"Don't wear that fucking dress."
"I'll wear what I fucking like."

EIGHT

1970

LONDON

The atmosphere was festive. The clocks had not yet gone forward and evenings were still dark, so the curtains were pulled and Thomas had lit candles around the living room to enhance the single side-of-the-room table lamp. He eschewed the harsh, central pendant when he was hosting one of his oft-held dinner parties, even with its regulation patterned scarf thrown over; it was not at all conducive to a relaxed, mellow evening.

He was in his element. The meal, cooked by his own fair hand, had been a success – as he was not shy, of course, of declaring; the dishes were Hungarian, with the rarer ingredients sourced from the specialist grocer he'd lately discovered in Notting Hill. Wine had flowed throughout the meal, *Egri Bikavér* or Bull's Blood as Thomas's favourite Hungarian red wine was known in England; but now the pálinka was out, and Thomas was once again holding court.

"Who did I have in my studio today?"

"I don't know," said András, wearily. "Who did you have in your studio today?"

"A rag-and-bone man! Is this how you say it?"

"Yes, that's right," confirmed Robert.

"But not any rag-and-bone man, a very special one!"

"In what way special?" asked Hazel.

"The most famous rag-and-bone man of all!"

"*Kedves Isten!*" exclaimed András, his irritation enhanced by the free-flowing alcohol. "*Kérem, mondja el nekünk!* Please just tell us, Tamás!"

"Thomas please, András!" his friend corrected.

"Thomas, Tamás, whatever! Which rag-and-bone man did you have in your studio?"

"Albert Steptoe," declared Thomas proudly.

"Albert Steptoe?" repeated Robert. "What, do you mean Wilfred Brambell, who plays him on television."

"In 'Steptoe and Son', yes," Thomas confirmed. "It is very funny."

"Was he funny today?" Hazel asked.

"No. He was very serious. He wanted photographs with no smiles, to get him good acting roles."

"I hope he paid you well," observed András, grumpily.

"He did," said Thomas with a smile, holding up his glass. "You are drinking some of the money he paid with now."

"Thomas! The rent is due on the flat at the end of this week!"

"And the studio comes due again next month," added Hazel.

"This month, next month!" said Thomas, waving his hands in the air. "We will have the money. Besides, Robert will be paying as usual at the end of the week also. Won't you, Robert."

"Oh, yes," said Robert. "Of course, as usual."

"*Így aztán*," said Thomas, with a shrug. "No problem."

"Though I'll be away for eight weeks after Easter, as you know," the young actor added.

"Eight weeks?" Hazel was surprised.

"Yes. I'm doing three plays in Chesterfield."

"Where is Chesterfield?" asked András.

"I'm not quite sure," Robert admitted. "The audition was in London. Up north somewhere, I think."

"It's near Sheffield, I believe," said Hazel. "Isn't it the town with the crooked church spire?"

"Crooked?" András was puzzled. "Why is it crooked?"

"I don't know," said Hazel. "But it twists up like a corkscrew. I've seen pictures of it."

"You English are very strange," András declared. "Why would you want a twisted spire?"

"I don't think it was built like that. It's just happened over the years."

"Strange! Very strange!"

"If you're going away for eight weeks, what about your room here?" asked Hazel.

"He will keep it, of course," Thomas announced. "Otherwise where will he go when he comes back?"

"That's right," Robert agreed.

"If he stops paying for eight weeks, I will have to find someone else for the room."

"No, no," assured Robert. "I'll keep paying the rent, don't worry. It's so reasonable, anyway. You're very good to me, Thomas."

"You think I should put your rent up?" asked Thomas, a sly twinkle in his eye.

"Oh, no!" said Robert hastily. "I'm not saying that. It's just about all I can afford, in any case, when I'm out of work. And I'll be back again when Chesterfield's over, looking for another job."

"Shish!" András exclaimed. "This acting! I could not live with it!"

"Robert loves it," defended Hazel. "Don't you, Robert!"

"Oh, yes. I love it."

"What plays are you doing?" she asked.

"Oh – er – three plays. 'The Homecoming'. It's by Harold Pinter."

"I saw it," Hazel said, "when it was in London, five or so years ago. It was excellent, so unsettling."

"Unsettling is excellent?" asked András, puzzled again.

"Of course it is," said Hazel, "in a play, or a painting, or any work of art."

"I like my art to be beautiful. I don't like to be unsettled."

"You are so ordinary, András," said Thomas. "You like your life normal, and boring."

"My life will never be boring," András said ruefully. "Not with you around – *Thomas*." He pronounced the name precisely.

"*Pompás!* Splendid!" declared his compatriot, triumphantly. "I would have it no other way!"

"'The Homecoming'," continued Hazel, "and what else?"

"Oh – er – 'David Copperfield' and then a comedy, a farce, 'Rookery Nook'."

"Oh, Robert! You'll have such fun!" said Hazel. "I'm so jealous!"

"You're mad!" Jenny shouted at her youngest daughter. "Quite mad. Tell her, Arthur."

"Well, it would seem to be a little impetuous. Are you quite sure, Brenda?"

"Of course I'm sure!" the girl said heatedly. "I wouldn't've said 'yes' otherwise, would I!"

"Well, you can't get married, can you?" went on her mother. "Not while you're only seventeen. Not unless I say 'yes' too."

"Then we'll just run away, won't we! We'll get married anyway, whether you say 'yes' or not. We'll go to – where is it? Where you can get married without your mum or dad agreeing?"

"Gretna Green," her "uncle" offered.

"Yes, thank you, Arthur," said Jenny through gritted teeth. "There'll be no running away, that won't be necessary. But can't you wait a while, Brenda?"

"Wait?"

"You might feel differently in a few years."

"A few years!" The girl was outraged. "No! I love him and he loves me. We're getting married now!"

"She does seem very certain, very sure of herself," Arthur said, when Brenda had stormed out, slamming the door, and Jenny and he were alone together. "If you're too negative on all this, you might risk losing her altogether."

"Of course I won't stop her, if she's absolutely determined. She's like me – or, rather, like I used to be. When she gets an idea in her head, there's no dissuading her from it. But, *Aidan?* I mean, honestly! Does she have no taste at all!"

"He's not the young man I would have chosen for her, certainly. But I suppose that's rather the point, isn't it."

"What is?"

"We're not the ones doing the choosing."

"You're right, of course. You always bloody are."

"Thank you." Arthur smiled.

"But all the expense, after Susan last year."

"I can help, if you need me to."

"No, no. It's not the money. It's just that I'm sure she'll be asking for a divorce in no time at all; before they've been married a year, I shouldn't be surprised. Living with someone is very different to meeting for a drink in a pub every now and then."

"Certainly."

The door opened and Wendy poked her head in.

"What's the row now?" she asked.

"Oh, just Brenda and Aidan again," said her mother, wearily.

"You might as well let her marry him," said her sister. "The sooner she's out of this house the happier we'll all be, if you ask me."

* * *

The pub was noisy and full of smoke. Brenda stood inside the door for a moment, scanning the room to see if she could spot Aidan. A man in a black donkey jacket moved away from the bar, carrying two straight pint glasses of beer, and she saw Aidan behind him, with his back to her, leaning on the counter, talking to another man she knew by sight but not by name. Aidan handed the man something, and the man handed him something back. She couldn't see what it was. Aidan shoved it quickly into his pocket, and the other man walked away from him, towards Brenda and the door. She looked him in the eye as he approached her.

"You want something, darling?" he asked her, not pleasantly.

"No," she answered, curtly.

"Careful who you're staring at, then," said the man.

She held his gaze for a few moments, then looked away. After the briefest of pauses, the man walked past her to the door and out of the pub. She looked back across to the bar again. Aidan still had his back to her, so she went across to him.

"Hi, lover boy," she said.

"Hi, beautiful," he said. He pulled her to him and kissed her on the lips.

She felt in his pocket and pulled out a small, white paper bag.

"Is this for me?" she asked.

"How did you know that was there?" he said, smiling.

"I'm magic. I can read your mind."

"I hope you bloody can't."

"I hope I bloody can."

"What are you drinking? Usual is it?"

"Yeah, cider, of course."

The barman gave Brenda a casual glance, when Aidan ordered the drinks. Well, she could easily be eighteen, kids looked so young these days. Besides, she was a regular.

NINE

1971

London

Thomas was excited. It was still the middle of the day, but he'd started drinking earlier than usual.

"We will make a film!" he declared.

"A film!" repeated Robert. They were in the flat together. It was a Saturday afternoon and András had gone out to see Chelsea play football.

"You are an actor, Robert," Thomas went on. "You will be in this film. You've been in films before."

"I… yes… well…" Robert faltered. "A tiny part in the last James Bond film, nothing really."

"*Pontosan!*" Thomas persisted. "You will be in this film. But first, you do a little job for me."

"Oh – er – little job?" Robert asked, nervous all of a sudden.

"It is difficult, you must understand. I cannot go back. They know me. But my brother and his family, they need things, things I can buy for them, little luxuries. We are so lucky here in England."

"You want me to go out to Hungary?"

"It would mean so much to them."

"And take some things for them?"

"Just a few little essentials, things they can't get back there. The authorities, they are so strict. They don't like people to enjoy themselves."

Robert was used to Thomas's sudden impulses, but this was the most radical he'd encountered yet. The idea of a trip to Hungary, behind the Iron Curtain, fascinated this young man, whose experience of the world didn't extend beyond Trowbridge and London, and a few short visits to two or three English regional towns and their repertory theatres, and a brief stint at Pinewood Studios near Slough. But this was out of the blue, a whole new ballgame.

"Won't it be dangerous?" he asked.

"Nem, nem!" the older man reassured him. "Besides, you are young, eh? A little adventure? A little danger? Why not! It will be fun!"

"I suppose," Robert conceded. Thomas was right, it would be fun. "Why can't you go yourself?" he asked, at length.

"It is impossible. I told you. I drove an ambulance, in the revolution. They would arrest me."

"That was fifteen years ago."

"They have long memories. I would be stopped at the border. I will come with you to Vienna, and then you take the train to Budapest."

"Behind the Iron Curtain."

"So you call it." Thomas's eyes twinkled. "My niece, she is pretty, no? You will like to meet her. So! I know you will."

Looking back, Robert couldn't quite work out why he'd

said a definite 'yes' quite so quickly, but he had. And so later that evening he found himself writing to his mother to let her know about this impending trip. And the following week he found himself packing a couple of smart new shirts, still in their cellophane, a sports jacket on its hanger, a few packets of tea, a jar of peanut butter, chocolates and several packets of filter-tipped cigarettes into a large suitcase, along with all his own personal clothes and toiletries for the journey.

He'd already called his agent, to make sure the next two weeks or so were clear for him, with no likely auditions imminent.

"Go, enjoy yourself," she'd said to him. "I'll have lots of lovely jobs lined up for you ready when you get back."

"I hope so," Robert had finished the conversation.

All the paperwork successfully arranged, the following Monday morning saw Robert trailing across the busy concourse of Victoria Station, as he tried to keep up with Thomas, who glided serenely ahead of him, and whose suitcase Robert lugged along as well as his own. They climbed into the train and worked their way along the corridor, until Thomas found an empty compartment and slid open the door. "This one will do," he said.

He settled himself down into a seat as Robert struggled in with the cases, and tried to lift one up onto the rack.

"Leave them on the seat," said Thomas, not quite a command, but Robert stopped struggling and settled himself down.

"I wonder if we shall leave on time," said Thomas.

"The train's not all that busy," Robert observed.

"The trains in Hungary were terrible. Here they are better."

They sat in silence for a while, and then Robert smiled.

"Will they let *me* in, do you think!" he said.

"You have your papers. We do it all by the book." Thomas took him seriously. "Of course they will let you in."

Robert was still smiling. "Ah, but will they let me out again!" he said.

The Hungarian allowed himself a sly smile. "Who knows!" he said. "Perhaps not!"

A guard's whistle sounded on the platform outside.

"Ah!" said Thomas. "We are off!" The train jolted into motion. "And so! The adventure begins, eh, Robert?"

Trowbridge

"Make mine a tea, too, Jen. Four sugars."

Aidan sat in Jenny's kitchen, waiting for Brenda to come back from the bathroom.

"Yes, your lordship," Jenny answered, sarcastically, and put the kettle on to boil. "So, have you found yourself a job yet?"

"Oh, I've got all sorts of jobs, don't you worry about that."

"I do worry, Aidan."

"Oh yes?"

"Not about you. About Brenda."

"Brenda's okay."

"Is she? Is she really?"

"She's fine with me. I'll look after her all right."

"I wonder." She took another mug from the draining board, banged it down noisily on the worktop and added a teabag. "When are you both going to move out of your mother's house?"

"Soon. I've got to talk to a bloke. He's going to organise something for us."

"Is he." Jenny's response wasn't a question.

She poured almost-boiling water into the mug and put it on the table in front of Aidan, without removing the teabag. He took a sip and pulled a face.

"God, Jen! Where's the sugar?"

"Oh, sorry," she said. "I forgot." She put the sugar bowl in front of him, and winced as he spooned four sugars into his mug, and then used the same sugar bowl spoon to stir it in. "I don't know how you can drink it so sweet," she said.

"Think I'm sweet enough already, do you?" said Aidan with a slimy grin.

"Oh no, don't worry, I don't think that," she said.

They both heard the downstairs toilet flush in the hall, and neither spoke again before Brenda came back into the room.

"All right, you two?" the eighteen-year-old said, sitting down at the table. "Been talking about me?"

"No, of course not." Jenny brought the kettle fully to the boil and made Brenda's tea.

"Your ma thinks I don't look after you properly," said Aidan.

"Mum!" Brenda protested.

"I didn't say that. I was only asking after your new house."

"Oh, Aidie's got all that in hand. Haven't you, love."

"That's what I was saying."

"Well, I hope so," said Jenny. She took the sugar bowl back from the table, put two spoonfuls into Brenda's mug with a clean teaspoon and stirred it round. "Here you are, dear," she said, putting the mug down in front of her.

"To be honest, I can't wait," said Brenda, warming her hands on the hot mug. "Aidie's mum is driving me round the bend."

"Here, Bren, steady!" Aidan protested. "There's nothing wrong with my mum."

"She thinks there's everything wrong with me. I can't do anything right for her."

"It's new for her, having a girl about the house. She's only ever had us boys before."

"Do you ever see your father at all?" Jenny asked.

"Don't want to see him," said Aidan, suddenly animated. "He'd better watch himself if I ever see him again. I'll fucking kill him!"

"Oh, Aidan, please!" said Jenny, shocked at the language, but not surprised.

"Take it easy, Aidie," Brenda soothed. "Your dad's long gone. He's never going to hurt you again."

"He never hurt me before! It's my mum he hurt. I'll never forgive him."

"No, darling. Quite right."

Jenny leant against the worktop and looked at them both, her youngest daughter, all grown up, and her daughter's dashing beau. It should all have been so different, she thought to herself, not for the first time.

"Come on, Bren," Aidan said petulantly, standing up. "We're going home."

"I haven't finished my tea yet," complained Brenda.

"I have," he said, and he left the room without waiting for his wife to follow.

"Let him go, love," Jenny said. "Stay and have your meal here."

"No, Mum." Brenda stood up too. "I'd better go or there'll be hell to pay."

"Brenda!" Jenny's heart was breaking.

"I'm fine, Mum. Don't worry." And Brenda went out of the house and chased down the road to catch up with her husband.

Germany

The train sped across central Germany towards Prague. The rural landscape scrolled past the carriage window. Robert and Thomas sat opposite each other in the dining car, eating soup.

"'The Third Man'," said Thomas suddenly, out of the blue.

"What about it?" said Robert.

"That is a great film."

"Yes, it is."

"Produced by Alexander Korda."

"That's right."

"From Hungary."

"Is he?"

"Yes. Of course."

"I see."

"If he can make a film," declared Thomas, "then I can make a film!"

Robert didn't know what to say to this, so they continued to eat in silence for a few moments.

"What will it be about?" Robert asked eventually, trying to kick-start the conversation again.

"Eh?" Thomas asked.

"The film, your film. What will it be about? Spies? The revolution?"

"*Nem, nem, nem!*" said Thomas, irritably. "Not spies! Not the revolution! I've had my fill of the revolution."

"Then what?"

Thomas's eyes glazed over, and almost filled with tears. "Oh, wonderful things!" he said. "Marvellous things! You will be amazed."

"I think I will," said Robert, unable to suppress a gentle smile.

"Oh, you will!" said Thomas, not noticing the smile. "It will be beyond your wildest dreams."

Robert turned his head to look out of the window. Thomas went back to eating his soup.

Delhi

It was odd how life changed. From the jaws of disaster five years ago, his circumstances had turned around completely. He sat on the veranda of his bungalow, enjoying a late afternoon gin and tonic. Perhaps his jowls were a little less taut than they had been five years ago, but he was comfortable, married, living in his own home, and his money worries were gone. Long gone.

"I'm ready, darling," a voice called from inside the bungalow.

He waited a moment or two, took another sip of gin, and then, "Good," he called back. "I'm on the veranda," he added.

His wife stepped out through the French windows. She was younger than him, by several years, slim, beautiful. She wore a light, delicately patterned flowing dress.

"Do come along, darling," she said, "or we'll be late."

"A few minutes won't make any difference."

"We're always late. *You're* always late. I'm forever hanging around for you. I thought it was supposed to be the other way around."

"Mm?"

"Men waiting for women, not women waiting for men. But, oh no, not in this household! Quite the other way around."

"Would you like a gin and tonic before we go?"

"John!" she expostulated. "We're going to be late!"

"Oh, all right." He gulped down the last of his drink and stood up, the hint of a troublesome lower back slowing him down by the merest second. "I just need to get my wallet. Have you got your bag?"

"Yes, of course. It's on the hall table."

"I won't be a moment, then."

He went into the bedroom and pulled open the top drawer of his bedside cabinet, and felt under the piles of neatly ironed and folded handkerchiefs for his wallet. He felt the butt of his revolver, too. He didn't need it now, but it was good to know it was there.

"Now do come on!" his wife said, as he joined her in the hall.

Vienna

The brakes began to screech and, with a kick of g-force, they felt the train suddenly start to slow.

"We are here!" Thomas announced. "Quick. Get the cases."

"Vienna?" Robert asked.

"Yes. Of course, Vienna. Get the cases."

Thomas had already slid open the compartment door, and was heading off down the corridor as Robert gathered their cases and tagged along.

The concourse of the *Wien Sudbahnhof* was quieter than Victoria Station had been, all those hours before. Thomas led him through the entrance and onto the street outside. It was evening now, and car headlights flashed as they motored past.

"Should we get a taxi?" Robert suggested. "Or a tram, is it?"

"*Nem. Nem*," countered Thomas. "I know the way. The hotel, it is not far." And he set off along the pavement, with Robert once again in tow.

Thomas was right. The little hotel he'd booked them into was not far away, and soon, having checked in and collected their room keys, Robert found himself standing in a second-floor corridor as Thomas unlocked his door.

"Leave your case in your room," Thomas said as the lock clicked and his door swung open.

"Right you are."

Finally taking charge of his own case, Thomas heaved it just inside the room and turned back to Robert.

"Knock on my door in ten minutes. I know a bar. We must celebrate!"

And with that he closed it sharply in the younger man's face. Robert stood still for a moment, taking in the fact that he was in Vienna, in the corridor of a shabby but clean little hotel, about to journey on behind the Iron Curtain into Hungary. Prior to this, Chesterfield had seemed like an adventure. He was born in India, of course, but that was so long ago, and he'd been so young when the family left for England that he could hardly remember it. He checked the number on his room key, and set off along the corridor in search of it.

* * *

The bar was heaving. Thomas had been lucky enough to find them both a small table in a far corner, and they each had a beer in front of them.

"What are we celebrating?" Robert asked.

"What are we celebrating?" The older man was already a little merry, and Robert suspected he'd been lugging a bottle or two of something or other around in Thomas's case all day.

"Yes. What?"

"We are celebrating life!" enthused Thomas, as he raised his glass to Heaven.

"Life?"

"Life! We are alive! Is that not cause enough to celebrate?"

Robert smiled. "I suppose," he said.

Thomas clicked his fingers. "Waiter! Waiter!" he called.

"What do you want?"

"Pálinka! We must each drink pálinka."

"I'll go to the bar," said Robert, half standing up.

"*Nem, nem!*" said Thomas, waving a hand to sit him down again. "There are waiters, they should come to us."

"They're busy," said Robert. "The place is full."

"A Hungarian is as important as an Austrian. Let them come to us."

"Thomas!" Robert protested gently, but his guide was determined.

"Let them come to us!" He clicked his fingers again. "Waiter! Waiter! Ah! One comes!" he said, as he saw a white-jacketed man approaching them.

"*Ja, bitte?*" asked the waiter, when he reached them.

"*Zwei gläser pálinka, kellner.*"

"*Jawohl.*"

The waiter turned to go, but Thomas stopped him.

"No. Bring the bottle, and two glasses," he said.

"Yes, sir," said the waiter without any intonation.

"I can't afford too much, you know," Robert said, when the waiter had gone. "We'd better take it a bit easy."

"*Soha!* Do not trouble yourself, Robert. You are a poor actor, I know. I will pay."

"You're not so rich, either."

"I do very well. I take many photos."

"I thought you said it was a bit quiet at the moment."

"I had a windfall. Don't worry yourself. Come! Drain your glass!"

Robert finished his beer, just as the pálinka arrived.

* * *

Next morning, they were back at the *Wien Sudbahnhof*. Thomas watched as Robert heaved his suitcase onto the train.

"You will give them the gifts," Thomas said.

"I will."

"And my love. Of course, you will give them my love."

"Yes."

"You have their photo."

Robert tapped his pocket. "I do."

"*Jó, jó.* You will recognise them."

"Yes."

"They will check your papers."

"Will they?" asked Robert, confused.

"The guards, the officials, they will check your papers."

"Oh. Right."

"Many times they will check your papers."

"That's fine."

"But you must not be worried."

"I'm not."

"They cannot arrest you. We do everything by the book."

A whistle sounded at the concourse end of the train.

"You are off!" declared Thomas. "Good luck!"

"Thank you."

The train started to move with a gentle jolt, and Thomas tried to keep up with Robert, leaning out of the window.

"I'll meet you here when you come back," he said, and then calling as the train left him behind, "In three days' time, I'll meet you here."

"Goodbye!" Robert called back to him, and then made his way along the corridor in search of an empty compartment. The train wasn't busy, and he soon found one to himself. He put his case up on the rack, and settled down by the window, watching the Vienna suburbs rattle past him. Soon his eyelids started to droop, and he allowed himself to drift off into sleep, grateful of the chance after the previous evening's pálinka.

Suddenly the compartment door slid open and a train attendant looked in.

"*Ihre Papiere, bitte,*" he said, brusquely.

"Sorry?" muttered Robert, still waking up.

"Your papers," the attendant repeated.

"Oh. Yes. Sorry."

Robert fished the bundle of papers out of his pocket and handed it to the attendant, who looked at them briefly, then handed them back with a curt "*danke*" before shutting the door noisily and moving on. Awake now, Robert stared out of the window.

TEN

LONDON

Hazel wasn't quite sure what to do with herself. For the first time in over ten years, Thomas wasn't around. Although she spent much of her time away from him, of course, somehow she always knew he was there, if she wanted to pop round to the flat or the studio; now, suddenly, he wasn't. She thought about going round to the flat anyway. András would just about be waking up, having something to eat, getting ready to go to work; he was on nights this week. She could spend an hour or so with him. But, on the whole, she decided, she'd rather not.

She looked around her bedsit. It hadn't changed in years. Some of the canvasses scattered around the room hadn't changed in years, still unfinished, still waiting for that final push. She didn't know why, but she'd lost her enthusiasm for it all. It hadn't happened suddenly. Just a slow, steady ebbing away of impetus, a draining of youthful exuberance, dragging her down to a life of monotonous spinsterdom, as the years were starting to drag down the features on her forty-year-old face. She looked at herself in the mirror, right up close. God, she was getting old!

She knew she must do something about it, something

positive, find some way to reawaken all her old energies, her old excitements. But how? She brushed her teeth at the kitchen sink, that always cheered her up. If only Thomas was here, he'd think of something. Or pour them all a drink. That was something she could do on her own, at least. She reached for a bottle, poured a drink and turned on the television, her tiny black and white portable. It was the time of day for children's programmes, and she settled down with a cushion on her lap.

Austria Hungary border

The train shuddered to a halt and Robert heard doors slamming. He opened the window and leaned out to look, but there was no station sign or even a platform he could see. He heard voices in the corridor behind him and turned to see two armed Hungarian border guards come into view through the glass. One of them slid open his compartment door.

"*Nyisd ki a bőröndödet!*" the guard demanded aggressively.

"Er…" Robert didn't understand.

"*Nyisd ki a bőröndödet!*" the guard repeated.

"I'm sorry?"

"Open your suitcase!" the guard said impatiently.

Robert sprang into action. "Oh! Yes. Of course." He opened up the suitcase, and the guard who hadn't spoken came into the compartment and rifled through its contents.

"*Documentumok!*" continued the first guard, while his colleague was searching.

"Right. Yes," said Robert, understanding, and feeling into his pocket again.

The guard snatched the papers almost before Robert had held them out, and scrutinised them closely, and then looked up at Robert suspiciously. The guard who was searching picked up the jar of peanut butter and showed it to his colleague.

"*Mi ez?*" the talkative guard asked Robert.

"Er…"

"What is this?"

"Oh – er – it's peanut butter?"

"*Mit?*" he asked again, aggressively.

"Peanut butter." Robert tried to explain. "Butter, made from peanuts."

The guard stared at him suspiciously for a moment or two, and then barked "*hagyja*" to his friend, who threw the jar back into the case. Leaving the case open, he searched under the seats of the compartment, while the first guard continued to scrutinise Robert's papers closely. At last, seeing his colleague was satisfied his search had produced nothing, he handed the papers back without comment and turned to leave.

"Thank you," said Robert, then, making an effort, "er – *koszonom.*"

The guard turned back abruptly at the sound of the Hungarian word, and looked hard at Robert again, but only for a second or two before going out into the corridor. His colleague followed, and shut the door behind them. They moved on down the corridor and out of sight, and Robert heard the next door slide open and the guard demand. "*Nyisd ki a bőröndödet!*" He put his papers back into his pocket, and started to repack the case more neatly.

Trowbridge

Aidan kicked the leg of the table.

"Don't do that, Aidie," Brenda protested.

"It's my table," he said. "I'll kick it if I like."

"It's mine too, love, and I don't like it."

"Your mum really gets my goat."

"I know, love."

"She treats me like scum."

"She doesn't mean to."

"Yes she does! She knows exactly what she's doing. She thinks I'm not good enough for you."

"Who cares what she thinks," said Brenda, putting her arms round his neck. "I think you're good enough for me. I think you're my shining prince."

"Don't be so fucking daft." He grabbed her wrists and shoved her arms away from him.

"It's not daft," Brenda persisted, embracing him again. "And you can't resist me, can you? You never have been able to."

"You're a witch," he said, and kissed her.

She kissed him back, and their bodies relaxed against each other.

"You can make me do anything," he said.

"Anything?" she asked.

"Anything," he said, and they kissed again.

Budapest

The Vienna train rolled into the platform of Budapest Keleti railway station. Robert was already at a carriage door, waiting to disembark. The platform was engulfed in steam and smoke, which wafted away from the side of the train as everyone threw open their carriage doors. He stepped down, clutching his suitcase close to his chest, trying to keep it safe amid the throng of all the other passengers pushing past him towards the exit. Gradually the crowd cleared, leaving behind it a light mist, a gentle memory of the previous pea-souper. Through this, distantly, on the far side of the platform, he caught sight of the most beautiful girl he thought he'd ever seen in his life. She was looking straight at him. As the final wisps of steam and smoke evaporated, the romantic in him thought he heard the second movement of Rachmaninov's second piano concerto playing somewhere, with full orchestra, up in the rafters of the station.

The girl came over to him. She was young, still very much in her teens.

"You are Robert Markham?" she asked.

"Yes. *Igen*," said Robert.

"Good," she said, and took a photograph out of her pocket. "From this, I know you," she explained. "You are very handsome."

"I… er…" Robert didn't know what to say.

The girl smiled at him, a warm, friendly smile, and he relaxed a little.

"And you are…?" he ventured.

"Maria. My name is Maria," she said. "I am Tamás's niece."

"Ah. Hello. *Szia.*"

"My father is János, his brother."

"Yes." Robert felt in his pocket. "I have a photo too. Of him. János. Your father. Thomas – I mean, Tamás – he gave it to me."

"Yes."

"He didn't give me one of you."

"No."

"Or one of your mother."

"It does not matter. I will take you to them." Maria smiled again and took Robert's arm. "Please, come."

* * *

Five minutes later they were standing inside a crowded tram, having failed to find any free seats, clattering through the Budapest streets. Maria leaned in close to Robert to speak to him, and he inclined his ear to hear clearly over the noise of the tram and the other passengers chattering.

"You must go to the police station," she said.

"Must I?" said Robert, alarmed.

"To have your passport stamped."

"Oh."

"Do not worry. It is normal. Everyone who comes to Budapest must do this. And again before you leave."

"I see."

They clattered on for a while without speaking, still close.

"We will be there soon," said Maria.

* * *

Maria unlocked the door at the top of the second floor stairwell.

"*Tessék*," she said, indicating for Robert to enter first. "Please."

A middle-aged man was just coming into the little hallway inside, having heard the door opening.

"Mr Markham?" the man asked.

"Yes. *Igen.* Yes," said Robert awkwardly. "*Kanizsa Úr?*" he asked tentatively. "Mr Kanizsa?"

"*Igen,*" the man confirmed. "*Üdvözlöm?*"

"Yes," said Robert, unsure.

"How do you do?" the man smiled, and shook Robert's hand warmly.

"Very well, thank you."

"I am Tamás's brother."

"Yes."

"János."

"Yes."

"He has told me all about you."

"Good."

"And you all about us, too, I am sure," he went on, still smiling.

"Yes."

"Please."

He led Robert into the living room of the apartment.

"This is my wife, Irina," he said, introducing the neatly dressed woman who was just coming out from a room at the back, which seemed through the open door to be the kitchen.

Robert held out his hand. "How do you do?"

"*Üdvözlöm?*" Irina said formally, accepting the handshake, though somewhat suspiciously.

"And my daughter, Maria, you have already met," János went on, with yet another smile.

"Yes."

"We are not very grand, I'm afraid," János said, as he took Robert's coat to hang it up.

"No, no," said Robert, looking around the room, which was spotless, but far from luxurious. "This is lovely."

"Lovely?" repeated Irina suspiciously, looking to her husband.

"*Szép, kedvesem,*" he explained to her.

"Ah," she said, seemingly satisfied.

"Let us listen to the radio." János went over to an old Bakelite wireless set, which had pride of place amid many little china ornaments, neatly dusted and arranged, on a dark wooden sideboard.

"Oh – right." Robert was a little puzzled.

János turned on the radio.

"It is good, the radio," Maria said.

"Is it?"

"Yes, it is good," her father agreed.

The set warmed up, and János turned the volume knob up louder than Robert thought necessary, a spoken word programme in Hungarian. He turned back to Robert.

"Then we can speak, no?" he said quietly. "Without anyone else hearing us."

"Anyone else?" Robert asked, at his normal volume, and Maria shushed him urgently.

"She's right, Robert," János said good-humouredly. "A little more quietly, please."

"Oh – sorry," Robert apologised, still not quite understanding. "*Sajnálom.*"

"It is better if no-one hears us," János explained.

"The neighbours?"

János shrugged his shoulders. "Possibly," he said.

"Anyone. It is best. So! Irina! Some food for our guest! Something to drink!"

"*Tessék?*" Irina asked, not understanding her husband's English

"*Gulyás. És pálinka,*" he said in Hungarian.

"*Igen, igen, tudom,*" she said, and bustled back into the kitchen irritably.

"My wife has prepared a wonderful meal, to welcome you."

"*Köszönöm.* There's really no need."

"Yes, yes. It is only right. *Gulyás.* It is good. Hungarian soup. You will like it. Now sit down! Sit down!"

Maria picked up Robert's suitcase. "What have you brought for us, Robert?" she asked.

"Maria!" Her father was shocked. "*Könyörgöm! Ne légy udvariatlan!* Robert is our guest."

"It's all right," Robert said. "Really. It's why I came, of course." He took the case from Maria and placed it on the table. "Oh – and to say that Thomas – Tamás is very well, and that he sends his love, of course." He opened it up and started to take out the things Thomas had sent for them. "Here. It's nothing, really. Just some tea, and chocolate. And peanut butter."

"*Ez csodálatos, csodálatos,*" said Maria, delighted.

"She says it's wonderful," János translated, and then went to the door and called softly, "Here! Irina! See what Robert has brought us."

"*Később,*" Irina called back from the kitchen, not bothering to keep her voice down. "*Most elfoglalt vagyok.*"

Robert took out the jacket and the shirts, and held them up. "I hope they fit all right," he said.

"It does not matter," János said. "Maria is right. It is wonderful."

With all the gifts extracted, Maria closed the lid of the suitcase. "I'll put this in my room," she said.

Robert was taken aback. "In *your* room?"

"Maria is sleeping in here," János explained.

"Oh! Please!" Robert protested. "*I* can sleep in here."

"No, Robert," said the girl.

"You are our guest," said her father.

Robert thanked them. The radio programme continued noisily in the background.

ELEVEN

Trowbridge

The birds were singing outside as Jenny sat at the little bureau in her bedroom and looked out over her garden. It had grown into a bit of a mess, now that Robert wasn't here to help with it, and Wendy – the only one of her children still living at home – had neither the inclination nor the ability to assist. It was all left to Jenny herself, of course – most things usually were.

She took a pad of blue Basildon Bond notepaper out of the bureau drawer, opened it up, and made sure that the loose, heavily lined insert was correctly placed beneath the top sheet; she never used the bleed-through of the lines to keep her handwriting straight, but it was useful to stop the indent of her biro going through to the sheet below. Jenny wasn't a habitual letter-writer, but there were certain old friends and acquaintances with whom she liked to keep in touch. She wrote regularly to her "Aunt" Rosalind, over seventy now and still living out in India; not a real aunt, of course, but someone who shared happy memories of past theatrical times, and who could give a flavour in her letters of a life she, Jenny, had once enjoyed.

Today, however, Jenny's letter was about business, to her

solicitor in London regarding some long-held family stocks and shares; he'd written to her last week about various future options, and a response with an opinion was required. Business, to Jenny, was a necessary evil; she needed the income it generated, and so liked to be very much involved in all the decision-making around it – well, she'd had to be, for the last twenty-plus years, since she'd been all on her own. She wrote her address in the top right-hand corner, her solicitor's name and address below it on the left, the date, and then began: "Dear Mr Wetherby…".

* * *

Aidan leaned the ladder against the brick wall, made sure it was safe, and started climbing. When he reached the roof, his head spun for a moment; surely this wasn't the best job for a man who suffered from vertigo, but Bren had insisted: "You've got to get a job!" she'd said. Aidan wasn't someone to be bossed around, but he knew she was right, and the chance had come along, working with an old mate. He was getting paid regularly, and not living off Bren's factory earnings all the time. That'd show the old cow, her mother.

His head cleared, and he cast an eye over the ancient tile-work in front of him. Yes, this lot was more than ready for a refit. He'd give the old couple a quote, what his mate had told him to quote, but with a little more added on to it, just for himself.

LONDON

Hazel had gone round to see András. She was at a loss as usual, and slightly merry, more so than perhaps was wise for the middle of the afternoon, but if it was all right for Thomas, then surely it was all right for her. András had been lying on the sofa in his underpants, and had hastily pulled on some jeans and a t-shirt when he heard the knock at the door. He let her in, and slightly reluctantly offered her a drink.

"Would you like tea," he asked. "Or coffee?"

"Have you any beer?" Hazel asked.

"Yes," he said, slightly surprised. "I think there's one bottle maybe in the cupboard."

"Then let's share it!"

"Oh, no," he hesitated. "I have work tonight."

"Half a bottle of beer won't hurt you."

"Won't it?"

"Surely not."

"Well. Okay."

András found the bottle opener and flipped off the top, pouring the beer into two glasses, one from the draining board and one from the cupboard. He measured them, and took care to put slightly more in Hazel's glass than his own. They sat in silence for a while.

"Are you going out this evening?" András asked at last.

"No," Hazel replied, adding, "Do you miss Thomas?"

"No," András answered, honestly. "I like having the flat to myself, and with Robert being away as well." He thought for a moment. "Do *you* miss Thomas?" he asked.

"Yes," she said. "I miss him very much." Perhaps the drink had made her speak so honestly.

Vienna

Thomas sat in a bar; where else. He nursed his glass, which had barely one sip left in the bottom of it. He was disappointed the bar wasn't more busy; just one businessman, engrossed in some papers with a coffee beside him, and a young couple, engrossed in each other. A pity, as he could have struck up a conversation with someone who was casually reading a newspaper. Even the waiter had been brusque, though polite, and the barman resolutely had his back to him, polishing glasses.

Conversation made the drink last a little longer, stretch a little further. He should really buy another, but just now he had to make his money last. It seemed a long time until he could meet Robert off the train from Budapest again tomorrow.

Budapest

Maria led the way down the stairwell and out into the street. Robert followed. It was a grey morning, but somehow Robert's mood was sunny.

"I will show you the important places," Maria said. "The – I do not know how to say it in English – the *híres* places."

"Famous landmarks," suggested Robert.

"*Igen.* Yes, that is correct. I will show you the famous landmarks."

"Thank you."

They walked along the pavement together, as Maria guided him to the tramstop, which they took into the centre of the city, then walking from the Parliament Building to the Hungarian State Opera – because Maria knew that Robert was interested in theatres – on to St Stephen's Basilica and across the Széchenyi Chain Bridge over the River Danube to Buda Castle.

"This afternoon we can go to the *Széchenyi Termálfürdő,* if you would like it."

"I'm sorry – the what?"

"I do not know how to say it."

"Well – what happens there?"

"There is water, hot water, from the ground. You can swim."

"Ah, I see. Like thermal baths."

"Thermal bath, yes, this is it."

"Good, good. Yes, that sounds good."

They walked on together, looking for somewhere Robert could perhaps buy them something to eat for lunch, and a little later they sat on a bench at the bottom of Gellért Hill, eating sandwiches.

"I enjoy this very much," Maria said.

"Yes, me too," Robert agreed. "They're nice sandwiches."

"*Nem.* No. I mean not only the sandwiches."

"No?"

"*Nem.* I mean sitting here, eating the sandwiches, with you."

"Good, I'm pleased," said Robert. "So do I – enjoy it very much – sitting here, eating the sandwiches, with *you.*" And then he added, "Would you like to come to England one day? I'd like very much to show you the famous landmarks in London."

Maria thought for a moment. "*Igen,*" she said, "*ez nagyon jó lenne.*"

"Oh," he said, unsure for a moment.

Maria laughed. "Do not worry," she said. "This means I think I would like to come to London very much."

Robert relaxed. "Oh. Good," he said, smiling.

TWELVE

1974

TROWBRIDGE

"Who's he bringing down?" Aidan asked abruptly. "What woman is this?"

"My big brother has fallen in love, I think," said Brenda. "He wants to introduce us to her."

"And she's foreign?"

"Yes. Hungarian or something, he said."

"They're Commies, aren't they?"

"I don't know."

"What's he want to go bringing a Commie into the family for?"

"I'm sure she's not a Commie."

"What do you know? Have you met her?"

"I'm sure she's not. Stop going on about it."

A sudden squawl emitted from the room next door.

"Now look what you've done!" grumbled Brenda.

"I ain't done nothing."

"You've woken her up."

"You woke her up."

"Only because I was talking to you."

"Oh, shut up! And shut that bloody baby up as well!"

"You shut her up!"

"I only make her worse."

"You're right there," Brenda agreed. "You're rubbish with her."

"You know what to do best."

"I do. Now are you going out to work or not?"

"Not till eleven."

"Why not? He hasn't laid you off, has he?"

"Course he bloody hasn't! I'm just taking it a bit easier this week."

"You take it so easy sometimes, Aidie, you might as well not get up in the morning."

"Will you shut it!"

"Well, it's true, isn't it?"

"I've got a lot going on at the moment, course I need my sleep."

His wife looked at him suspiciously. "What've you got going on apart from the roofing, then, Aidie? Tell me. I need to know."

"Oh," her husband hesitated, "just this and that, you know."

"No, I don't know. Are they legal, these this and that?"

"What d'you mean 'legal'?"

"You know very well what I mean. You've got a family now, Aidie. We've got little Sharon."

"Don't I know it!" Aidan expostulated as the squalling went on next door.

"It's not just me now. You're earning for all three of

us. Get yourself put away and Sharon and I'll be right in it."

"Will you go and shut that baby up!"

"I'm not going crying to mum if that happens."

"Good!"

"She's helped us out enough already."

"Bloody interfering old cow!"

"Don't you talk about my mother like that! We'd've been lost without her these last few months."

"We'd've managed just fine."

"Well, go to bloody work, then! And I mean proper work, not dodgy deals round the back of the pub with God knows who."

"Oh, leave it, will you?"

"Yes? Do you get me?" said Brenda forcefully as she left the room.

The baby was red faced and screaming as her mum lifted her out of the large black and chrome pram Jenny had bought for them – much to Aidan's annoyance.

"There there," Brenda said, patting little Sharon's back and holding her close. "Nothing to be sad about, just your silly old dad and mum going on at each other. There there."

She swayed from side to side, from foot to foot, gently rocking the baby, and gradually the crying quietened, and then finally stopped with a little gurgle.

"That's better, isn't it," Brenda cooed. "All that nasty crying, that don't do any of us any good, does it?"

She heard the front door slam hard, and Sharon threatened another protest.

"There there," Brenda patted and rocked, nipping it in the bud. "That's just your gumpy old dad going out to do

God knows what with his dodgy mates. Don't let us take no notice of him. There there."

Mother and baby stood there, happily close to each other, for a good half an hour, before it was time for another feed.

London

"We go on a trip!" Thomas enthused. "Into the English countryside. I am enraptured!"

"It's not really the countryside," Robert corrected. "Trowbridge is quite a large town."

"But we travel through the countryside, do we not? To get there?"

"Not necessarily. We could drive down the new motorway, till just past Swindon. I looked it up."

"But this new motorway, it goes through countryside?"

"Well, yes, I suppose it does," Robert conceded.

"Exactly!" Thomas triumphed. "We travel in the English countryside."

They were all in the Kensington flat: Thomas, Robert, András, Hazel and Maria, who was on her second visit to London to see Robert. András had made tea, which they were all drinking, except Thomas, who chose to leave the tea cup beside him untouched, nursing instead a glass of pálinka between his hands. Every time he took a sip, his niece Maria would throw him a disapproving look, and utter a barely audible tut, which Thomas either failed to hear, or, which was more likely, ignored.

"Must this journey be next weekend?" András asked.

"It's when they're all off work, apparently," explained Robert. "It's the best time to get them all together."

"This is a pity," András complained. "This weekend I do a double shift, so I won't be able to come with you."

"Nobody invited you anyway," Thomas declared. "You will not be missed."

"Oh, don't be so mean, Uncle," said Maria reproachfully. "Of course András could come with us. Couldn't he, Robert?"

"Well, yes, I suppose so, if he wasn't working."

"And Hazel, too, if she would like," Maria continued.

"Oh, no," said the elder woman. "I'd only be in the way. You three go on your own."

"But you must come," said Maria.

"The thing is," Robert intervened, "as we're staying overnight, well, I suppose there might only be room for three of us."

"Of course," said Hazel. "Much better for just you two to go with your uncle."

"Well, we shall miss you, Hazel," said Maria. "And you too András."

"Yes," said Thomas. "Hazel would have cheered us all up."

"I'm very much looking forward to meeting your mother, Robert," said Maria, changing the subject, "and your sisters, Susan, Wendy and – er…"

"Brenda," Robert helped out.

"Yes, Brenda. And her husband is…?"

"Aidan. He's – er – he's quite a character is Aidan."

"I look forward to meeting him. And Susan's husband is…?"

"Peter. He's a doctor."

"That's a very good job."

"Yes."

"What does Aidan do?"

"Oh – a little bit of everything, I think. I'm not quite sure. I think he's doing a bit of roofing at the moment."

"That too is a good job," chimed in Thomas.

"Oh?" queried Robert.

"Everyone needs a roof," Thomas explained. "Like you gave us a roof, Hazel. Me and András. When we first arrived in England all those years ago. You were so kind to us."

"Oh – well…" said Hazel, embarrassed.

"No," András agreed, "you were so kind."

* * *

The sun was bright in the autumn sky when Robert, Maria and Thomas set off on their expedition to the West Country. Robert drove his newly acquired third-hand Ford Anglia car, with its reverse slanting rear window, and Thomas sat beside him, with Maria in the back. The M4 motorway had not long been open, and was not very busy, so they bowled along unimpeded at a happy 50 miles per hour. The radio in the car had long ceased to function, well before the car had belonged to Robert, and the three travellers, after chatting cheerfully through the outskirts of London, had settled into a comfortable engine-hum silence.

Just after Reading Robert turned the car off the motorway and drove around trying to find somewhere for lunch, as it was now well after one o'clock. It was Thomas who spotted the pub sign a little further down the lane, and suggested they park up there. It was a pleasant, oak-beamed affair in the traditional style, which pleased Thomas no end, though the variety of food available was severely limited: pork pies, of course, which Thomas scorned, packets of crisps and two or three varieties of sandwich. Thomas settled for a packet of cheese and onion crisps, but was happy enough with his double whiskey, the pálinka option having been explored and found, as expected, to be unavailable; Robert and Maria shared a rather uninspiring round of cheese sandwiches; and Maria sipped at a glass of lemonade, while Robert enjoyed a half of malt-brown fizzy bitter.

Lunch achieved, such as it was, they set off again, rejoined the motorway, and, an hour or so later, with the sun low in the sky in front of them, found themselves turning off the motorway and driving south towards Chippenham, Lacock and Melksham.

The sign for Trowbridge revealed itself, much to Thomas's delight, and Robert navigated easily to Brenda and Aidan's house. Brenda had seen them draw up, and was already halfway down the front garden path to meet them when they started getting out of the car.

"Hello, big brother," Brenda greeted Robert, with a smile and a brief but sincere hug.

"Hello, Bren," Robert replied, happy to see his sister again.

"And who's this?" Brenda asked with a twinkle, as Maria joined them.

"This is Maria," Robert introduced. "She's over from Hungary, visiting for a week or so."

"Hello, Maria," said Brenda, formally shaking hands.

"I'm very pleased to meet you," said Maria.

"And this is Thomas, Maria's uncle," Robert went on, as Thomas walked up the path.

"Oh, I've heard all about you!" Brenda said, with a knowing smile at the dapper emigré.

"All bad, I hope," grinned Thomas.

"Yes, yes," said Robert. "I can't think why you two haven't met before – I've known Thomas for quite some time now."

"Enchanted," said Thomas, taking Brenda's hand in a gallant, antique fashion.

Just then, Aidan emerged from the house.

"What's all this noise out here then?"

Brenda quickly pulled her hand away from Thomas. "It's Robert and his friends, of course," she said. "Who do you think it is!"

"I don't know," grumbled her husband, "could've been the milkman."

"Don't be daft!" Brenda scolded.

"Hello, Robert," Aidan greeted his brother-in-law sullenly.

"Aidan," Robert replied, with exaggerated cheerfulness. "Good to see you. This is my friend Maria."

"Hello, Robert's friend," Aidan said to Maria.

"Hello, Aidan," Maria replied, a little perplexed at this slightly aggressive greeting.

Robert went on, "And this is Maria's Uncle Thomas—"

"And your landlord, Robert! And your friend!" Thomas added, flamboyantly.

"Yes, exactly," Robert agreed, slightly embarrassed at Thomas's effulgence.

Aidan grunted a rude acknowledgement to the older man and turned back to the house. "Sharon's screaming," he informed his wife without looking at her, and disappeared back inside without another word.

"I can hear that for myself," Brenda called after her husband.

Indeed, they all could hear, for an insistent squalling had started up a few moments after the young mother had left the house.

"Come along inside," she invited them all. "I'd better see to the little horror – and I'll put the kettle on for a cup of tea. You must all be dying for one."

"Dying, yes!" exclaimed Thomas. "For tea?" He left his interrogative hanging in the air.

They all trouped inside and Brenda showed them into the neat front sitting room. Aidan had already plonked himself down in his usual chair in the corner.

"I'll just go up and settle her," Brenda said. "I've only just put her down for a sleep, but the voices must've woken her."

"All this bloody noise," said Aidan.

"May I see her?" Maria asked.

"Oh, yes, of course." Brenda sounded pleased. "Do come up with me, Maria."

The women left the men alone in the room. Robert sat down, while Thomas roamed up and down, his eyes searching none too surreptitiously for some sign of a drinks tray, or a cabinet.

"How's work, Aidan?" Robert asked, trying to keep the social niceties bowling along.

"Work's work, ain't it," the younger man replied curtly.

"Is there enough coming in?"

"Too much."

This avenue of conversation firmly shut down, Robert tried a different tack.

"We had a good journey. Came on the new motorway – the M3. It was quite quick, wasn't it, Thomas?"

"What's that?" Thomas asked, distracted from his alcoholic musings.

"The motorway – it was quite a good way to come."

"Ah, yes, yes! A lovely drive through the English countryside!"

"Christ!" said Aidan, to no-one in particular.

"Have you driven on it yet?" Robert asked.

"Ain't got no car, have I!" rejoined the other.

"Oh, no, of course not."

"And Mikey only lets me drive the van for work."

"Yes, I see."

"So I wouldn't've driven on it, would I!"

"No, I'm sorry. I didn't think."

"No, you didn't, did you."

This put an end to Robert's attempts at small talk, and they all three remained silent for a while. The crying had stopped a few moments ago, and shortly Brenda led Maria downstairs again, the baby contentedly in her mother's arms.

"What's up with you lot, then," she said, as she found them all sitting mute, "cat got your tongues?"

"You have a lovely baby," Maria told Brenda.

"You can have her if you like," the other quipped.

"Oh, I – er…" Maria did not understand.

"Only joking," explained Brenda, kindly. "You're right, she's gorgeous. Can't imagine how, with parents like she's got! I'll put the kettle on."

"The kettle, yes," Thomas mused. "Or perhaps something a little stronger?"

"You'll be lucky!" laughed Brenda. "If there's anything

stronger in the house, it's drunk before it's been here five minutes – and not by me, I hasten to add."

"Will you stop going on," her husband complained. "I can't do anything right, can I!"

"Oh, you're not so bad, when you try."

"I will treat you to something nice to drink," said Thomas.

"Thank you very much, Thomas," said Brenda.

"And I will cook for you tonight, a beautiful meal."

"That's all right. Mum's coming round in a while, and she's bringing a casserole."

"Then I will make a pudding! Is that right? A pudding? Something sweet to follow this magnificent casserole."

"Well, if you like," said Brenda.

"Christ!" Aidan muttered again.

* * *

Jenny arrived an hour later, delivered by her recently acquired unofficial chauffeur, William, an acquaintance from her part-time job at a local estate agent's.

"I won't come in," he said, as he opened the car door for her to get out. "One new girlfriend or boyfriend is enough in one day."

"Who says you're a boyfriend?" Jenny remarked, coquettishly.

"Well, I'm your friend," William smiled, "and I'm a boy."

"Fifty years ago, maybe," Jenny smirked.

"Even so." He paused for a moment, and then added, "If one of them doesn't run you home, just give me a call."

He waited in the car until he saw Brenda open the front door to her mum, and then drove off.

"You should've asked William in," said her daughter. "We've got quite a houseful today."

"He has things to do. So what's this girlfriend of Robert's like?"

"She's lovely, and she's in the front room listening to every word you say! Come in and say hello."

Robert stood up when Jenny entered the room; Aidan sat sullenly, without so much as a glance in his mother-in-law's direction. Maria stood up too and Robert introduced her.

"This is Maria, Mother," he said. "I've told you all about her."

"You have," said Jenny.

"Mrs Markham," said Maria, holding out her hand formally, "I am very pleased to meet you."

Jenny took the proferred hand and held it briefly.

"You're a long way from home," she said as she let the hand go.

"Yes," said Maria. "My family live in Budapest, which is in Hungary."

"So I understand."

A muttered noise came from the direction of Aidan's chair, which no-one could quite make out, but which might have contained the word "Commie".

"What's that, my darling?" Brenda asked her husband sweetly. Her husband declined to enlighten her.

"I know a lot about being far from home," Jenny said. "It's been my experience for many, many years."

"But I thought you lived here, in Trowbridge, Mrs Markham," said Maria.

"I was born in India. I was brought up in India."

"Ah, yes, I understand. Robert has told me."

"I was married there. I had my children there."

"Mother misses India very much," Robert explained.

"I was happy there."

"And you're happy here, too, aren't you!" said Brenda, lightening the mood. "You haven't met Robert's friend Thomas."

"Oh, yes, of course," said Robert, hastily. "This is Thomas – Maria's uncle and my landlord in London."

"I am extraordinarily pleased to meet you, Mrs Markham," said Thomas extravagantly, taking Jenny's hand and kissing it, whether she liked it or not, which, from her expression, it seemed she didn't.

"Yes, well, I understand you've been very kind to my son since he's been in London," she said, reclaiming her hand hurriedly, "for which I thank you."

"It is my pleasure to help my friend, and my honour," Thomas acknowledged, with a flourish of his newly released hand. "The people in London were very kind to me when first I came to England."

"Thomas came over to London after the Hungarian uprising, Mum," said Robert.

"Yes. You told me."

"A terrible time, a time of bloodshed and heartache and broken families," Thomas expanded.

"Yes," Robert said awkwardly.

"Still it is bad there."

"It is not so bad, Uncle," Maria chided her uncle. "My mother and father are happy there."

"Ach!" full-stopped Thomas, as if nothing more need be said on the subject.

All introductions completed, a moderately pleasant evening was enjoyed by all, and the spirit of the whole company was lifted when Aidan went out to meet a mate about some business that needed his urgent attention. Thomas did indeed comandeer Brenda's kitchen to create a pudding, much to the young woman's amusement, and her mother's irritation, though the resulting confection was admired by all, particularly Thomas himself. When the festivities were over, Robert drove his mother home, while Brenda settled Maria in her room and checked on baby Sharon, and Thomas sat forlornly nursing a small glass of cooking sherry, the near-empty bottle of which had been unearthed from the back of a kitchen cupboard.

Delhi

His wife sat across the starched white tablecloth from him in the corner of the club's dining room. She was eating the last few scrapes of chocolate mousse from a small glass bowl. He had declined pudding, ever more aware of his gently widening midriff – how the years took their subtle, almost imperceptible toll.

He still thought her beautiful, that was undeniable, but something about her demeanour was beginning to annoy him. The way she grated her spoon against the glass of the bowl to harvest every last scraping of the mousse set his nerves on edge, and the tiny smear of chocolate on her upper lip disgusted him.

"You have a…" he left the words hanging as he waved a finger vaguely at her mouth.

"Thank you, darling," she acknowledged, and wiped the

offending smear away with her linen napkin, already soiled from other necessary wipes during her previous course. "All better now?"

"Yes," he replied. "All better."

Though of course it wasn't. His life had become irritable again, and he wasn't sure how much longer he'd be able to put up with it.

THIRTEEN

1978

TROWBRIDGE

The light had barely started to dispel the all-pervading night of the wood as Aidan parked the van up a dirt track in the little clearing. He was unused to being awake at this time of the morning, let alone being out and about, preferring the warmth of his bed, while his wife tended to baby Sharon and returned with a mug of sweet tea, which often remained untouched on his bedside table. Indeed, Brenda had woken with a jolt when he had eased himself out from beneath the sheet and blankets in the darkened room.

"Where are you going?" she asked him, surprised and bleary.

"Go back to sleep," Aidan had said, trying to dismiss her concern.

"No, Aidey – where are you going?"

"Just a bit of business," Aidan said.

"Oh, no, please!" Brenda pleaded. "It's not light yet – what business do you need to do this early?"

"You knew what business I did when you married me," Aidan hissed.

"Oh, shit, Aidan! For fuck's sake!" She was awake now. "You've got a good job. You don't need all this crap on the side."

"This crap pays for your life."

"It pays for your drinking."

"Go back to sleep," he said again, an order this time.

"How can I? You worry me to death."

"I can look after myself. You worry about Sharon."

"I do! And you! She wants her dad."

"She's got her dad," he said, and it was a full stop to the hushed argument.

Brenda watched as he pulled on his pants, jeans and t-shirt, and hunted around for socks.

"Put a jumper on," she said, "or you'll freeze out there."

"I'm fine," he said.

He found the socks, sat on the bed to slip them on, and then went to the door.

"Will you be back for breakfast?" Brenda asked.

"Might be. Might not. Might go straight on to work."

"Aidey?"

He turned back to her, something in her tone of voice stopping him in his tracks.

"Yeah?"

"Be careful."

He smirked, and went out of the room.

There was no-one around he could discern when he climbed out of the van. The air was crisp and cold and his breath smoked in the half-light. He climbed back into the van, turned on the light and checked his Timex wristwatch

– 5am – that was right, he was bang on time. He sat for a moment in silence, wondering if he'd got the right clearing, but the instructions had been easy and he had no doubt he'd followed them correctly.

The complete quiet of the wood was starting to suffocate him, when he heard the gentle drone of a car engine in the distance. It grew ever louder, and Aidan climbed out of the van again to greet the occupants of this new arrival. The light from its headlamps swelled from two dots until they almost blinded him.

A smart Hillman Avenger crackled over the frosty leaves and drew to a halt beside the van. The lights and engine snapped off, and suddenly the dead silence of the wood engulfed Aidan once again. But not for long. Both of the car's front doors swung open, and two figures climbed out. They each shut their respective doors smoothly and came towards the young man. Neither of them were much older than Aidan, but their bearing suggested a greater worldliness, a greater confidence.

"Aidan Harvey?" said the one on the left, the one who'd been driving. His voice was low, rich, no Wiltshire accent, maybe a hint of something foreign; Aidan couldn't work it out.

"Yeah."

"You've passed the first test," the man on the left went on.

Foreign, yes, definitely something foreign.

"Oh yeah? And what's that?"

"You found the right place. You arrived on time."

"Yeah, well, that's me, ain't it! Reliable."

"I hope so."

For a moment, he said nothing more. The man on the right stood still, also saying nothing. Eventually, Aidan broke the silence.

"Shacky said you might have some work for me."

"Shacky," repeated the man on the left.

"Yeah, Shacky – in The Black Swan. He said he'd set up this meeting. He said there might be big money in it for me."

"Big money," the man on the left repeated once again. "You would like big money?"

"Yeah! Of course! Wouldn't everyone?"

"Some people are maybe content."

"Well I'm not – I want more."

"Greedy."

"No – ambitious."

"That's good."

"But *are* you?" The man on the right spoke for the first time, a cut-glass English accent, almost aristocratic.

"Am I what?"

"Reliable."

"Reliable! Yeah! Ask Shacky."

"Shacky," repeated the man on the left yet again. "Well, we must see."

The man on the left explained a few details, imparted a few instructions, to which Aidan nodded submissively. The man on the right didn't speak again. The meeting over, the two men climbed back into the car and its headlights lit Aidan starkly as the engine sprang purringly into life. The car reversed round sharply and then drove off steadily back up the dirt track.

Aidan stood for a moment, taking in what had just

happened. Then he too climbed back into his vehicle, started up the engine and turned around to drive back the way he'd come. It was lighter now, and although technically headlamps were still needed, he didn't risk them, as he drove back into Trowbridge to make an early start on the roof that currently occupied his daylight attention.

Bromley, Kent

"Have you got your sandwiches?" Maria asked, as Robert clicked shut his smart new briefcase.

"Yes, thank you."

"And your flask."

"Yes, but there's a kettle in the office at the back. It's not really necessary."

"They may not wash the cups properly."

"Mugs, there are mugs."

"Whatever – they might not be washed properly."

"I'm sure they are – I often wash them up myself."

"Ah. Well. The flask can do no harm."

"No. It's lovely. Thank you."

Robert kissed Maria on the cheek.

"I love you," he said.

"I love you too," she answered, meaning it.

"What will you do today?"

"I may make a start on the little room at the front – it needs painting."

"Yes, well, be careful."

Maria smiled at him, a warm, loving smile. "How can I hurt myself with a paintbrush?"

"Well, if you stand on a chair, or something."

"I'll be careful. Now go – or you'll be late."

She waved him off as he walked down the path and through the gate, and then watched till he reached the corner with the High Street. He turned back to wave himself, just before he disappeared out of sight towards the bus stop, and then she went back into the house.

* * *

Robert looked around the back room of the bank. This was not how it was supposed to be: married, nine to five, with a little house in the suburbs. By now he should've been famous, well known and respected within the acting profession – at least, that was how his mother had envisaged it panning out for him. And he hadn't done badly: he'd worked, he'd had some nice jobs, he'd earned money. But perhaps history repeats itself. Long gaps between contracts on benefit doesn't provide a stable basis for a young couple wanting to start a family, and Maria wanted children, Robert knew she did – and he wanted to be with her, like she wanted to be with him. It was an easy decision to make, and he could always go back to it later, when things were more established.

The wedding in Budapest had been an extraordinary, rather wonderful affair, overcast by the prevailing atmosphere of conditions behind the Iron Curtain, and by Irina's reluctance and suspicion; but enlivened by János's enthusiasm and support, and by Maria and Robert's determination and love for each other. The decision to leave Hungary for England was a life-changing one for Maria, so brave, and Robert respected and loved her all the more for it. A small, smart terraced house in Bromley on the southern outskirts of London couldn't have been more different from a second-floor apartment in the suburbs of Budapest.

The telephone rang and his boss answered it.

"It's for you, Markham," he said, holding out the receiver. "A foreign gentleman, I believe. As quick as you can. You know I discourage personal calls at the bank."

"Yes, of course, Mr Jenkins. I'm sorry. Thank you."

Robert recognised the voice at once.

"Thomas! I've asked you not to call me here."

"I know, I know." The rich Hungarian accent crackled down the line. "But until you get a telephone installed in your tiny new house, how else do I contact you?"

"You could write a letter."

"So long! I need to tell you now. I am having a dinner party tonight. You and Maria must come."

"Oh, I don't know—"

"Of course you must. András misses you, so does Hazel, she is coming too."

"But Maria is cooking at home."

"It can wait. You can eat it tomorrow, your cheese on toast."

"No, I don't think—"

"I must see you tonight. Any time after eight – and bring a bottle of pálinka."

There was a click and the dialling tone in Robert's ear before he could protest any further. He replaced the receiver glumly. He knew Maria wouldn't want to go to Thomas's that evening; neither, really, did he, though deep down he somehow missed the exuberance of living with the erratic emigré. He'd call at lunchtime from the telephone box on the corner and ask her, but he knew already the answer, and could envisage the subsequent call, telling Thomas they weren't coming. Why hadn't he just said "no" straight away! Well, he wasn't really given the chance, was he? That was Thomas all over. Robert sighed and settled down to a column of figures.

Of course Maria didn't want to go, and of course Thomas was theatrically insulted. But it would blow over, and one day soon, when Maria had a little more warning, they would go and visit her uncle.

LONDON

"Do you miss him?" Hazel asked.

"Do I miss who?" retorted Thomas.

"Why, Robert, of course."

"Miss him? Miss Robert? No, of course I don't. Why do you insult me like this!"

"It's not an insult," Hazel said reasonably. "He lived here for some time; you were close, you were friends."

"We still are. Besides, I am busy. I take pictures, I plan a movie. I have no time to miss Robert."

"He does, of course," said András, from his chair in the corner. "So do I. Robert was a nice person to spend time with."

"But we are back as we were, no?" exclaimed Thomas. "We are back as we began, the dynamic threesome! Thomas, András and Hazel! Always Hazel – we could not imagine life without you."

"Oh," the woman blushed. "I don't know. I don't think I could imagine life without you, Thomas – or András too, of course."

The younger man smiled.

"To us!" declared Thomas, brandishing his glass in characteristic fashion.

"To us!" the other two repeated, and they all felt the thick, sweet pálinka warm the backs of their throat.

Trowbridge

"And so my boy is married," Jenny wrote. "Not the life I would have chosen for him. Not the wife I would have chosen for him, perhaps, but he seems happy enough. I don't really understand."

She paused for a moment, pen in hand, and looked out at the garden. She'd tidied it for the winter as well she could, and even Wendy had given a hand. Brenda had offered, but Jenny had turned her down – she had quite enough to do with Sharon just starting school, and that ghastly husband of hers doing nothing to help. William had also offered, and she had let him light and manage the bonfire for her.

A car horn sounded in the street at the front of the house. Jenny sighed and wrote a couple more sentences before signing off. She licked and sealed the wafer thin, pale blue airmail letter and slipped it into her bag. They could stop by the pillar box at the end of the road as William drove them both to lunch at their favourite café.

FOURTEEN

1980

DELHI

A great sense of relief overwhelmed him. He was free once again, and all achieved so neatly. No need for the revolver in his bedside table, much simpler than that. An accident – well, the Delhi roads were so dangerous, and if the brakes on your car were even the slightest bit faulty – well! He knew if his wife had merely been injured there'd be more work to do, but she was killed outright, a fatal collision, no need to rush her to hospital, she was pronounced dead at the scene. He couldn't have been happier – inside.

Outwardly, of course, he was distraught, a husband broken by the loss of his beloved wife. He even managed to express sympathy for the young man driving the other car involved, paralysed by the crash, a promising career as a doctor shattered – such a tragic waste of a life. It would take him some time to get over his distress, naturally, and those around him were very supportive; he couldn't have asked for better friends and colleagues.

As the weeks and months passed, they thought they saw an improvement in him, as he began to talk about the future, about making a fresh start. He needed a change of scenery, he said, maybe even some time away from India. He'd been abroad before, several times, on holiday, but had always lived in Delhi; now, perhaps, in his unarguable middle age, it was time for a new adventure. He wouldn't rush into anything, but it was certainly worth considering.

Inside, of course, he knew exactly what he was going to do.

Trowbridge

The argument was not a new one, but this time it was worse.

They'd gone round to Jenny's for Sunday lunch, as they occasionally did; Brenda hopeful, Aidan reluctant and Sharon excited. Jenny loved to see her six-year-old granddaughter, so lively and full of fun, and – her nana hoped fervently – with a bright future ahead of her, far away from the mundanities of life in Trowbridge. How Jenny hated being called "nana"! It put her in a bad mood from the offset, despite her best intentions to stay cheerful and uncritical for her daughter's sake.

William was in the kitchen, washing up, now very much a fixture at these family gatherings.

"Why don't you marry him," Brenda had said to her mother a couple of years ago, "or, if you don't want to get married, just live with him."

"Brenda!"

"Well, he's always round here, and you do like him."

"Things are fine as they are, thank you very much. There's no point in messing around with them."

"If you say so, but it'd save William a fortune in petrol and shoe-leather."

The roast lamb and apple crumble and custard had passed without upset, in spite of Aidan's innate sullenness, and they'd moved into the sitting room with a cup of tea.

"It's a pity Wendy's not here," said Brenda.

"Oh, she's hardly ever here now," said Jenny. "I think she's got a boyfriend, not that she'd ever tell me anything about it."

"Wendy with a boyfriend!" Brenda laughed, though not unkindly. "I can't imagine it."

Aidan muttered something under his breath.

"What's that, darling?" Brenda asked. She was smiling, but there was an edge in her voice.

"Nothing."

"There's not much point talking if you've nothing useful to say," Jenny observed.

"Why don't you help Sharon set up the farm?" his wife said quickly, before Aidan could snap back at his mother-in-law.

Jenny had kept a few of the children's toys from when they were little, and Sharon loved playing with them whenever they went round. Today she'd chosen Brenda's box of plastic farm animals, with the farmer and his wife and all the fences and trees, and she was laying them out meticulously on the green rug in front of the fireplace. At her suggestion he should join in the game, Aidan looked at his wife as if she was mad.

Jenny went on, "My father used to say that. 'Never speak unless you've something useful to say'."

"Mum," Brenda warned.

"And he didn't," Jenny persisted. "He was a very wise man, my father. I know!" She jumped up from the settee.

"What, Mum?"

"I've got an old photo album somewhere." She opened one of the sideboard cupboard doors.

"Christ!" said Aidan, under his breath.

"No, Aidey, they're fun. I used to love looking through those photos when I was a kid."

"Here we are." Jenny took a dark blue mottled album from under a pile of knick-knacks at the back of the cupboard. "I haven't looked through this for ages.

She sat down again beside her daughter and they started turning the pages.

"There's your grandfather," Jenny said, pointing to a picture. "And there."

"Doesn't he look smart in his uniform! And that's him with Granny, isn't it?"

"Your grandmother, yes."

"Come and look at these photos, Sharon," Brenda encouraged her daughter, "they're of your great nana and grandpa. Imagine that!"

"Leave her be," said Aidan. "Can't you see she's happy playing?"

"Well, you have a look, then, darling. They're lovely, all brown and white and faded."

"No thanks."

"Suit yourself." Brenda turned a page. "Who's that? You have told me, I know, but I can't remember."

"That's your Uncle Wilfred."

"He's in uniform too."

"He fought in the Boer War before he went to India. Most of the men in our family were in the army back then."

"Load of stuck-up gits!" Aidan grumbled.

"Load of stuck-up gits!" Sharon mimicked, giggling, and without interrupting her game.

"Sharon!" Brenda protested. "You mustn't say that!"

"Daddy did," said her daughter, reasonably.

"Aidan, honestly!" Brenda turned on her husband.

"Well, they are!" he said.

"There's nothing stuck-up about the army, Aidan," Jenny said. "It's a proper career, it's secure. You should think about joining up, young man."

"Mum, for goodness' sake!" Her daughter could see how this was going.

"Me! Join the army!"

"It'd do you good."

"Fuck off!"

"Aidan!"

"I'm not shocked, Brenda, if that's what he wants."

"But in front of Sharon."

The little girl giggled.

"Don't you dare!" her mother forestalled her.

"At least you'd earn some proper money," Jenny persevered.

"I'm doing all right for money just now, don't you worry! Ain't I, Bren?"

"Yes, I suppose," Brenda said uneasily. "Yes."

"I mean proper money, Aidan. A regular salary, so my daughter and grandchild can be cared for properly."

"I look after them okay."

"What? With the scattered earnings of an occasional roof tiler!"

Aidan stood up, furious. "You old bitch!"

"Aidan!" Brenda objected, but she knew it was too late.

"Well, that's very nice, I'm sure," said Jenny.

"Come on, Bren!" Aidan grabbed his wife's wrist.

"What?"

"I said, come on!"

"You're hurting me."

Sharon started crying.

"Then come on! We're leaving!"

William came in, wiping his hands on a tea towel. "What on earth's going on in here?"

Aidan ignored him. "I said we're leaving!"

"But Sharon's in the middle of her game. It's all right, love, don't cry."

"The old bitch can look after her."

"Oh, now, now, now!" William scolded. "There's no need for that."

"And her fucking toyboy."

Brenda was almost in tears herself. "Aidan, please!"

"You hurt my daughter in any way and I'll have the police down on you so fast your feet won't touch the ground."

Aidan let go of Brenda's wrist. "Come on, Bren!" he pleaded, near to tears himself and pushing past William to get out into the hall.

"It wouldn't be the first time you've spent a night in the cells," Jenny called after him.

"Look after her, Mum," Brenda said, "we'll just go outside for a moment."

She followed Aidan out of the room. He'd left the front door open for her, and was sitting behind the wheel of his latest battered van. She climbed in beside him.

"For fuck's sake, Aidan!"

"I can't take it anymore! That old bitch of a woman making out I'm the dirt on her shoe!"

"She doesn't think that."

"She bloody does! I can't bear to be near her anymore!"

"Let's go home and calm down a bit."

"I can't bear to be in the same town as her."

"What? Don't be daft."

"Let's go. Let's go anywhere. Let's go and stay with Robert."

"Aidan!"

"He'd love to see his little sister."

"Robert's away – they're visiting Maria's family in Hungary with the baby."

"Shit!"

"Just come back inside, eh love?" Brenda tried to soothe her husband.

"I know!" There was a sudden wild fire in his eyes. "We'll go and see his Uncle Thomas."

"What!"

"He's a friendly bugger."

"You're mad!"

"He'd love us to stay."

"This is crazy!"

"And he's got a spare room, now Robert's moved out."

"We can't take Sharon all the way up to London now," Brenda reasoned. "Besides, she's got school tomorrow."

"Leave her with her sainted nana, then. You're always saying you'd like a break."

"Yes, but—"

"We're going, Bren." There was a scary determination in his voice. "I've made up my mind."

Brenda sat silently for a moment, she knew this mood of Aidan's. "I'll go and tell Mum," she said at last. "You turn the van round."

When Brenda went back into the front room, Sharon had stopped crying. William was kneeling on the rug, helping the little girl set up the farm; Jenny was still flipping through the photograph album on her lap. Brenda explained their plan, expecting her mother to object, but she just smiled a knowing smile and said how much she'd enjoy spending some proper time with her granddaughter. She could sleep in Brenda's old room, she said. William didn't say anything, though he probably thought much. Brenda hugged Sharon and explained that she and Daddy were going away, just for a day or so, and that they both loved her very much, and that she should be a good girl for her nana. Sharon looked ready to cry again, but William distracted her by asking where he should put the plastic cow.

"Take care," he said to Brenda, when the little girl was once again absorbed in the game, "and call us any time you need to. You've got my number as well as your mother's. Isn't that right, Jenny?"

"Of course," said Jenny, her attention mainly on the album.

Brenda climbed back into the van, Aidan revved the engine aggressively and they stuttered off down the road leaving a cloud of exhaust fumes behind them. At his wife's insistence, they stopped off at the house to collect a few things for themselves, and, much to Aidan's disgust, drop Sharon's school uniform and a few clean clothes back round to her grandmother's, and then they set off towards the M4 and London.

KNIGHTSBRIDGE

András looked at his watch. Eight o'clock, near enough.

Time for another tour round the department store, just to check everything was all right, as it always was. He'd been working here for over twenty years, and the worst he'd ever had to deal with was a leaking fire hose, or a broken window. Sometimes he wished he might stumble across a burglar, trying to steal some ties from menswear, or maybe even televisions from the electrical department; but, then again, on the whole, probably best not.

Sundays were the worst. The end of a long weekend shift, in the large store, all on his own for forty-eight hours. Still, he got off at 11 pm when his colleague would arrive to take over.

He liked his regularly required tours round the store, looking at all the things – most of which he'd struggle to afford – looming ghostly grey in the dingy emergency light: huge piles of tins and boxes of biscuits in the food hall, where the smell of cheese from the humming refrigerated display counters was all-pervasive; life-size cardboard cut-outs of the latest action figure above the actual boxed figures in the toy department; manikins in the clothes departments; potted plants in the restaurant. It was another world, a night-time world.

Half an hour or so later he was back in the little office he shared, Box-and-Cox-like, with his colleagues. He'd filled the kettle in the men's room just along the corridor, and now he plugged it in again and put a teabag into his mug. Tinny-sounding music was issuing softly from the little transistor radio on the shelf. He wasn't keen on Radio Two on a Sunday evening, it was rather too melancholy for his taste, but somehow he couldn't bring himself to turn it off.

He made the tea, picked up the Sunday newspaper and

settled himself down in his chair to reread the gossip he'd already read several times before that day.

KENSINGTON

A loud banging on the street door below him, and an insistent ringing of the doorbell that sounded inside the flat, woke Thomas from the forty winks he'd been enjoying in his armchair, a siesta that had drifted on longer than expected, thanks to the assistance of a healthy dose of after-lunch palinka. He gathered his bleary thoughts together, grasping somehow that Hazel was no longer in the room with him. She'd washed and dried up, and had obviously decided to let herself out of the flat when it became clear her idol wasn't going to stir from slumber for some considerable time.

The door was still being hammered when Thomas reached the bottom of the hall stairs. "All right! All right! I'm coming!" he called out, and shuffled across the diamond-patterned tiles to turn the latch. Aidan stood on the step, looking harassed and irritable.

"We don't want to buy anything, thank you," Thomas said.

"Thomas!" said Aidan. "Don't you recognise me?"

"Jesus Mary!" Thomas exclaimed, when he'd looked at his visitor more attentively. "What are you doing here?"

"It's a long story, Thomas. Can I come in?"

"Robert doesn't live here anymore. He's moved to Bromley." Thomas pronounced the word "Bromley" deliberately and with some distaste.

"I know."

"But it's no good you going there now, because he is in Budapest with my niece, his wife, and their new baby."

"I know. It's you I've come to see."

"Me? What in Heaven's name for?"

"Please," the young man pleaded.

"You'd better come inside."

Aidan followed Thomas up the stairs and into the flat.

"What is this is all about?"

And so Aidan explained how he couldn't bear to be near his mother-in-law, and how he and Brenda had driven to London on impulse.

"Please can we stay with you tonight? You've got a spare room, haven't you?"

"Yes, but…"

"We're desperate, Thomas. There's nowhere else we can go."

"Where is your lovely wife now?"

"She's sitting in the van outside."

"Well, bring her in! Bring her in!" the elder man exclaimed. "Don't leave her on her own outside in the cold!"

"Thank you, Thomas!" Aidan said warmly. "I really appreciate this."

"Bring her in!"

Aidan went hurriedly out to the van and came back a few moments later with a reluctant-looking Brenda in tow.

"Hello, Thomas," she said.

"My dear," enthused Thomas, "it's a delight to see you here."

"Listen, Aidey," Brenda turned to her husband, "I've changed my mind. I don't want to be away from Sharon."

"Ah! Your charming little daughter," said Thomas. "How is the sweet little thing?"

"She's fine, thank you," said Brenda. "She's with her nana."

"Her nana?" Thomas was confused.

"Her grandma, I should say. But I don't like being away from her, Aidey."

"Well, I'm not staying in Trowbridge tonight. I've said, haven't I?"

"Then you go back, Brenda, and Aidan stay here," suggested Thomas practically.

"I can't drive, can I?" Brenda explained.

"I'm not staying back there," Aidan repeated.

"So then why not bring the dear little thing here," Thomas suggested.

"Oh, I don't know…" Brenda faltered.

"It would be a pleasure to see her again."

"She has school tomorrow."

"Pff!" exclaimed Thomas, dismissively. "School! A day or so will make no difference. Say she has a cold, they will believe you. This is good. Aidan, you drive back to Trowbridge and collect your daughter. You do not need to stay there. We will telephone ahead of you and the little girl will be ready to come."

"All the way there and back tonight?" Aidan was decidedly unsure of this plan of action.

"It is the only way," Thomas insisted. "I will take care of your wife while you are away. And we will put on our thinking caps to see what we can do."

Aidan turned to his wife. "Bren?"

"I want Sharon with me," she said, simply.

"Right then," Aidan said, decisively. "Look after her, Thomas. I'll be back as soon as I can."

He and Brenda shared a perfunctory hug, before Aidan went out of the flat.

"So, my dear," said Thomas, smiling. "We have a telephone call to make."

* * *

Jenny did object to this latest suggestion.

"This is madness, Brenda," she said down the phone. "She's in bed now, fast asleep. She's had a bath and a story and she's perfectly settled. No. I won't allow it."

"I want her, Mum," said her daughter simply, "and Aidey won't stay in Trowbridge."

"Aidan is a spoilt child."

"There's no arguing with him when he's in this mood."

"Then it's about time someone stood up to him."

"Please don't, Mum!" Brenda begged. "You'll only make everything a thousand times worse."

There was silence at the other end of the phone.

"Please. I want Sharon with me. Don't you understand?"

More silence.

"Is William still there?" Brenda asked, eventually.

"William went home hours ago, Brenda. I can deal with Aidan Harvey on my own, don't you worry about that."

"Just let him collect her, Mum. It'll be exciting for her. It'll be an adventure."

"It'll be upsetting and disruptive. Missing school on a father and mother's whim! I never heard of such a thing."

"No, I'm sorry, Mum. I'm insisting, and that's all there is to it."

"You're as bad as him sometimes, you know, Brenda. I really don't understand you at all. What do you see in the man?"

Brenda wasn't about to enter into that recurring argument again over the phone. "Aidan'll be with you between nine and ten—"

"I'll probably be in bed myself by then."

"Just have Sharon ready for him."

"Brenda!"

"Thanks, Mum." Brenda hung up, before her mother could say anything more.

"She wasn't happy?" asked Thomas, who had been hovering in the background.

"Not entirely," said Brenda.

"You are right! It will be an adventure for the little girl. She will remember it for the rest of her life! Now, we must make you feel at home. Would you like something to drink?"

"Oh, er, a cup of tea would be very nice, thank you."

"A cup of tea!" Thomas was amused in his outrage. "A cup of tea! You English people, you are obsessed with your cups of tea!"

"I'm sorry, I…" Brenda was confused.

"Very well! I will make you a cup of tea, and then you will have a glass of pálinka with me. That is a proper drink."

"Oh, I don't know…"

"I insist. You will like it. It will make you feel warm and not so worried."

"Well, if you say so. Thank you."

* * *

Hazel poured herself another glass of sherry, which had grown to be her tipple of choice when she was alone in the bedsit. She was used to sitting there on her own, and although she didn't much like it, it was preferable, somehow, to listening to Thomas snore for three or more hours on end, with András out at work. Awake, Thomas was the best company she had ever shared; asleep, he was just like any other man. Not that she had much experience of other men sleeping to make this comparison with any firm conviction.

She had traded in her little black-and-white portable television for a larger, colour model; and she quite enjoyed the new antiques programme that was on on a Sunday evening, but that was about it. She preferred the radio, Radio Four ideally, and could drift off contentedly, if not happily, to a murmur of meaningless words in a miasma of sherry fumes.

Half an hour later she was challenging Thomas with the volume of her snoring.

* * *

A stressful day and several shots of pálinka, which Thomas encouraged his anxious visitor to knock back in one, had almost had a similar effect on Brenda; she too was near sleep on the little sofa. She looked across the room and it suddenly started swimming.

"Oh God!" she exclaimed to herself quietly, "I don't feel very well."

"Then it is time for bed," said Thomas. "Come, I will take you to bed."

"What?"

"I will help you." Thomas went over to Brenda and tried to lift her off the sofa.

"What are you doing?" she slurred, not understanding.

"It's all right, my dear," he said trying to get his hands round her waist, "I just want to take you to bed."

"Get off me!" Brenda struggled to free herself. "You dirty old man, get off me or I'll scream."

"What, my dear?" said Thomas, surprised, not understanding what was wrong.

True to her word, Brenda screamed, loudly.

"All right, all right!" Thomas stood away from her, holding up his hands in submission. "My God! I wasn't going to hurt you. Honestly, darling."

"Just you fucking try!"

"I was only helping you to bed."

"I can make my own bloody way to bed thank you. Plying me with drink so you could have your way with me."

"So I could do what?"

"Shag me, you bastard!"

"I do not understand."

"Yes you bloody do!"

"No. I swear to you."

"Lay a finger on me and I'll kill you."

"I will not touch you. I promise. I was just trying to help you stand up."

"I can stand up myself, thank you very much," said Brenda, doing so unsteadily. "I'm going to bed. On my own!" She stood uncertainly for a moment. "Where is it?"

"I will show you."

"Yes. But keep away from me."

"Don't you worry, my dear. I will!"

Thomas led her along the corridor to the spare room. He put his hand round the door frame to turn the light on, but stepped aside back into the corridor to allow Brenda to go in. She closed the door behind her without another word.

"Sheesh!" Thomas exclaimed, under his breath, once he was alone. "What was that all about?" And he went back into the living room to tidy away the cup and saucer and one of the pálinka glasses.

* * *

András checked his watch again; it was gone half-past eleven. Really, Mike Rodgers was taking liberties. Nobody minded if you were five minutes or so late for your shift, but half an hour or more was beyond a joke. Much longer and András would have to make another tour of the store himself. He sat, bolt upright in his chair, mug washed up on the shelf, radio still playing.

Five minutes later, Mike Rodgers arrived, full of apologies. "Sorry, mate," he said when he appeared at the office door. "Lame excuse, I know, but I overslept."

"Do you not have an alarm clock?" András asked the young man, without any hint of humour in his voice.

"Ha!" Mike laughed, treating this as a joke. "I'll give you an extra half an hour, I promise, next time you take over from me."

"You do not need to do that. Just do not be late next time."

"I promise!" Mike took off his coat. "Cross my heart and hope to die," he said, suiting the action to the word. "Anything to report?"

"No. Nothing. All quiet." András already had his coat on. "Goodnight, Mike."

"Sorry again, mate," Mike called after him down the corridor. András didn't answer.

* * *

It was just about midnight when the doorbell rang again in Thomas's flat. He had been sitting up in the chair, waiting, enjoying occasional gulps from his glass between dozes. He went downstairs and opened the street door, where Aidan was standing holding a fast-asleep six-year-old in his arms.

"Bless the little one," said Thomas, quietly. "Bring her in."

"Lay her down on the sofa," he said, when they were back inside the flat; his words were soft, not quite a command, but Aidan behaved accordingly.

"Where's Bren?" he asked.

"She is asleep in her bed. We must not wake her."

But Brenda had heard the hushed voices.

"Is she here?" she asked, as she came along the corridor, still fully-dressed, and recovered a little from the pálinka thanks to an hour or so's sleep. "Oh, my darling!" She saw her daughter asleep on the sofa and went over to stroke her gently on the forehead.

"Do not wake her," warned Thomas. "She is sleeping happily."

Brenda turned to her husband. "He's a pervert!" she hissed, under her breath. "He tried to hit on me."

Aidan was confused. "What, Bren?" he asked, trying to take this in.

"This dirty old man you were so desperate to come and stay with, he tried to hit on me, while you were away. He made me drink a horrible drink, and then tried to take me to bed."

"Is this true?" Aidan hissed angrily, turning on Thomas. "Did you try to hit on my wife?"

"I do not know what you mean. What is this 'hit on her'? I haven't hit anyone."

"Don't try and be all la-di-da and clever with me, you Commie bastard!"

"He had his arms round me, Aidey."

"I'll teach you to hit on English girls, you pervert!"

Aidan swung a fist at Thomas, which, more by luck than judgement, the older man avoided.

"Don't, Aidey!" said Brenda. "Let's just leave."

But Aidan had already embarked on another swing and this one struck home, sending Thomas reeling onto the floor, and narrowly missing hitting his head on the table. He lay on the rug and groaned.

"My God!" he exclaimed loudly.

This woke the little girl, who, although she didn't see her father hit Thomas, sensed something was wrong in this new and unfamiliar room. She started to cry.

"Get up, you bastard, and let me hit you again!" went on Aidan, though his adversary was in no fit state to take to his feet.

The door opened, and András came in, home from his night shift, and intending to have a quick hot drink before climbing into bed. He stopped in his tracks when he saw the tableau before him: Sharon crying, Aidan with clenched fists shifting his weight furiously from foot to foot, Brenda torn between restraining her husband and egging him on, and Thomas sprawled on the floor beside the table.

"I'm gonna kill you! You'll see what happens when someone hurts my wife."

"I didn't hurt her."

"You tried to get off with her."

"'Get off'?"

"I'm gonna kill you!"

András went to the phone, picked up the receiver, and dialled 999, without saying a word.

"Aidey," Brenda warned, seeing András do this, and picking up the crying child from the sofa.

"I warn you." Aidan held his clenched fists close to his sides. "You watch yourself whenever you go out at night, because one day I'll be waiting for you, in the dark, and I'll kill you."

"Police," András muttered into the phone.

"Come on, Bren!" Aidan ordered, and he turned on his heels and marched out of the flat without waiting to see if she followed him. Brenda looked quickly from one to the other Hungarian, and then hurried after her husband, Sharon still in her arms.

Briefly, András explained to the voice at the other end of the line what he'd seen, and they said they'd send someone round immediately. He replaced the receiver, closed the flat door Brenda had left open behind her, and went over to Thomas.

"Can you get up, my friend," he said, putting his arms around him. "Here, come and sit on the sofa."

He helped Thomas to stand up, shakily, and take the two or three steps needed to sit down. Then he went to the kitchen and poured out a healthy glass of brandy, from an unfinished bottle at the back of a cupboard, bought in desperation a year or so ago when the shop had run out of pálinka.

"Here. Drink this," he said sitting down beside him.

"Ugh!" Thomas exclaimed after his first sip. "What is this!"

"It's brandy."

"Ugh!"

"It will do you good. Drink it."

Thomas obeyed, gumpily, like a reluctant child forced to eat their greens.

"Who were those people?"

"It is Robert's sister and her husband. They came here earlier, wanting to stay. I said no, but they insisted."

"And did you?" András asked, after a moment's pause.

"Did I what?"

"Try to make love to his wife?"

"No! No! I offer her a little drink, to make her welcome. She feels unwell. I try to help her to her bed in the spare room. That is all."

"You must tell me everything. The police will be here soon."

BERKSHIRE

Sharon snivelled as she sat between Aidan and Brenda in the front of the van.

Her father stared straight ahead of him, gripping tightly to the steering wheel as he made his fourth journey along the M1 in the space of the last ten hours. He forced himself to concentrate on the red tail lights of the cars in front, staving off tiredness and the uncontrollable impulse of his eyes to drift shut. His anger helped him stay awake.

Brenda had her arm around Sharon, and was too tired and confused to say anything. The young mother just wanted to be back at home, with her daughter tucked up in her own bed. Nothing could be said just now that would make this situation any better; that could come later, if it had to.

Ten minutes after, the snivelling stopped and Sharon was asleep. They drove on through the night.

Kensington

True to their word, the police arrived promptly, a sergeant and a constable, both in uniform, who politely asked the two émigrés to explain what had happened. András told them what he had seen when he returned to the flat from work, and then started to tell Thomas's story for him.

"It might be better," said the sergeant, "if Mr Kanizsa gives us his account of the incident himself."

"Yes. Of course. I'm sorry," András apologised.

"Not at all." He turned to Thomas. "That is, as long as you feel up to it, Mr Kanizsa?"

"*Igen.* Yes."

"You weren't seriously injured by the assault, sir?"

Thomas rubbed his cheek. "My jaw aches as I have never known," he said, "but it is still in one piece."

"Do you think perhaps you should visit the Emergency Department to have it checked over?"

"*Nem, nem, nem!* I will be perfectly fine after a night's sleep." Thomas didn't add "and after another slug of pálinka", though he thought it.

"So, sir?" the sergeant prompted, and Thomas proceeded

to relate the events of the evening, from Aidan's first arrival at his doorstep, to the final punch and death threat.

"And you were present for this death threat, were you, Mr Lovász?" the sergeant asked.

"Yes, absolutely," András confirmed. "He said it twice. He said he would wait in the dark for my friend and kill him."

The sergeant made another note in his pocket book, and went on, "Do you wish to press charges against this gentleman, Mr Kanisza?"

"Charges?"

"For assault."

"*Nem!*"

"No," András translated.

"I never want to see him again!"

"Yes, well, in that case," the sergeant made a final entry in his notebook, "as this Mr…" he referred to his notes, "Mr Aidan Harvey?"

"I believe that is his surname, yes," Thomas confirmed.

"As Mr Harvey is no longer present, there's little more we can do on this occasion. I'll make sure a full report of the incident is on record, and should you ever hear anything further from Mr Harvey, please make sure you let us know at once."

"Don't worry! I will! I don't want to end up with a broken arm, or leg, or worse."

"I very much hope it doesn't come to that, sir." The sergeant stood up. "Well, thank you very much, gentlemen. The incident must've been very upsetting for you both."

"Upsetting! Pfff!" exclaimed Thomas, in indignant confirmation.

"Quite," concluded the policeman. "We'll say goodnight to you now, then, gentlemen."

"Goodnight officer," said András, "and thank you."

"Goodnight," said the constable, who had stood up throughout and now spoke for the first time.

When they were on their own again, András turned, concerned, to his friend. "Are you all right, Tamás?"

"*Igen*," the other confirmed grumpily.

"Really?"

"I say so, don't I!"

"*Jó*. Then I will go to bed."

"Go! Go! I will not be long after you."

TROWBRIDGE

The Harveys were sleeping in, even though it was a Monday morning. They'd arrived home just after two, Aidan too tired and angry to worry about the proximity of his mother-in-law. Brenda had carried her sleeping daughter inside and tucked her, fully dressed, into bed; there was no question of her going to school later on, she'd phone and say Sharon was sick, though off her own bat, and not because Thomas had suggested it earlier. She and Aidan had climbed into bed themselves and lain, a little apart, not touching; within minutes, they too were fast asleep.

It was their turn to be woken by a sharp knocking at their front door.

"Aidan," Brenda prompted, trying to wake up.

"Let them knock," Aidan said, rolling away from her.

But the knocking was insistent. "I'll have to go," Brenda said at last, getting out of bed and putting on her dressing gown.

"Morning, Mrs Harvey," said the policeman on the doorstep. "Is your husband in?"

Brenda looked from one to the other of the two uniformed men in front of her. "What's wrong? What do you want?"

"Is he in?" the policeman persisted.

"He's in bed."

"Very cosy. We'll come in, if we may, and you can call him down."

"What's this all about?"

"Just call him down, will you?" The policeman walked past her into the hall, without any ill will, and his colleague followed suit. "In here, shall we?" the first policeman asked, indicating the front sitting room.

"I suppose," said Brenda, sulkily.

"Call him, will you?"

Brenda went back upstairs and shook her husband. "Aidey. It's the police."

"What?"

"They want to see you."

"What? Why?"

"I don't know, do I? They've let themselves into the front room. You'll have to come down."

"Shit!" Aidan struggled out of bed and threw on yesterday's clothes.

"Morning, Aidan," said the first policeman cheerfully, when the young man came into the room.

Aidan recognised the two visitors. "Morning, Sergeant Hopkins, Constable Maisley. What's all this about, then?"

"Were you and Mrs Harvey in London yesterday evening?"

Aidan paused a moment, before answering, "Might have been."

"Were you?" the policeman insisted.

"Yeah," Aidan said, looking down.

"And you visited a Mr Thomas Kanizsa?"

"He's my brother's wife's uncle," Brenda explained.

"Very complicated. I understand, Aidan, that you assaulted Mr Kanizsa."

"Did I?" said Aidan, insolently.

"Apparently so. You also threatened to kill him."

"Well, he deserved it!" Aidan burst out, getting angry again. "He hit on my wife."

The sergeant turned to Brenda. "Is this true, Mrs Harvey?"

"Yes," she said, hesitantly.

"You don't sound very certain."

The drive home last night and a few hours' sleep had clouded Brenda's initial judgement of the incident. "I think so."

"Do you mean, he attempted to rape you?"

"Well – kiss me, maybe?"

"I see."

"He deserved it," Aidan reiterated.

The sergeant paused for a moment, thinking.

"You're lucky, Aidan," he said at length. "Mr Kanizsa doesn't wish to press charges."

"Bloody right he doesn't!"

"But I'd strongly advise you never to see him again, or make contact with him in any way."

"I don't want to, don't you worry!"

"Or you'll find yourself spending a lot longer in jail than the odd night for a fight in a pub, like you've been used to."

Aidan didn't answer.

"Do I make myself clear?"

The young man shrugged. "Yeah," he said, as if it wasn't important.

"Well, mind you don't. Mrs Harvey?"

"He won't." Brenda reassured the sergeant, "I'll make sure."

"Good. Good morning to you both, then. Have a pleasant day."

The two policemen left the house, the constable having been silent for the entirety of the visit.

"Come on," said Brenda, when she'd closed the front door on them, "I'll make some tea and we can go back to bed."

"No," said Aidan, "I'm up now. I'm going out."

FIFTEEN

1981

MAYFAIR

He laid his suitcase on the neatly made bed and clicked it open. It had been a long journey, and all he wanted to do now was to have a bath and lie down for an hour or so. The liner had been comfortable enough; he was, of course, travelling first class, and he'd chosen the month-long sea voyage over a day by plane, both for the relaxation and also to avoid all the hassle and security he envisaged at the airport. But the journey up from Southampton in a cramped, smelly train compartment had taken its toll on his touchy constitution, and although the five star hotel on Park Lane was a welcome sight in itself, sleep between crisp, clean sheets was his ultimate goal, even though it was only three o'clock in the afternoon.

The bath was almost filled by the time he'd shared his clothes between the chest of drawers and the wardrobe; he could unpack the bits and pieces in the bottom of his case later. He undressed, climbed in and felt his muscles relax as the steaming hot water engulfed him. He tried to clear his mind, but myriad different thoughts tempted him.

Truly events couldn't have worked out better. It was high time to leave India behind, there was nothing left for him there, but how perfect to do so without any encumbrance. He had enjoyed his various liaisons, but certainly didn't want them to last for an eternity. Now he was fancy-free, believed innocent, and six and a half thousand miles away. No financial worries, either, thanks to a few lucky business years recently, and a healthy life insurance payout.

When he was towelled and dry, he slipped on the silk pyjamas he'd left ready, and distributed the remaining contents of his case around the room: alarm clock beside the bed, and so on. He put the case beside the wardrobe and slid between the sheets. Before he drifted off, he picked up his address book from beside the alarm clock and flicked through the pages.

Yes, there were old acquaintances with whom he really must get in touch.

BUDAPEST

"But we *have* to go, Mama," Maria protested in Hungarian. "We've been here two whole weeks."

"Two weeks!" Irina grumbled. "I don't see why you can't stay longer. What is so special about England?"

Maria sighed. "Robert has to go back to work. He's used up all his holiday this year."

"A bank clerk! I thought he was an actor."

"He was."

"And how are you going to look after the baby, with your husband out at work all day?"

"How did you look after me as a baby, when Papa was out at work?"

"I was older than you. I was more responsible."

"Nonsense! You were exactly the same age. Besides, I have friends in Bromley, and we have Robert's family."

"Pfff!" Irina sounded unimpressed.

"You can 'pfff!' all you like, Mama, but we still have to go. The tickets are booked. It's the eleven o'clock train."

Robert understood snatches of this exchange between mother and daughter in their native language; he'd picked up a fair few Hungarian words and phrases from Maria over the last ten years, but he was far from fluent.

"*Sajnálom*," he said apologetically to his mother-in-law. "I'm sorry. It's my work. There's nothing I can do."

Still unimpressed, Irina "hurrumphed" out into the kitchen, just as János had emerged, drying his hands on a towel, having washed up the breakfast things.

"Don't worry about your mother," he said softly in English, over the constantly playing radio underscore, and with a smile to Robert. "She misses her daughter, that is all."

"Well, I miss her," said Maria, also in English.

"Of course you do. But with the little baby girl as well – well, she wants to see her grow up."

"She will."

"She fears she will miss something. And as we are not permitted to leave Hungary and visit you—"

"We'll come as often as we can," offered Robert. "All my holidays are devoted to it."

"I know," said János, smiling again. "You are very good, both of you. Now come on, wake little Christine from her morning nap, or you will miss that train. Irina!"

he called into the kitchen, and then went on in Hungarian. "Come and kiss your granddaughter, and wish her a happy journey."

Trowbridge

"I don't want it," said Brenda resolutely.

"They're real diamonds," said Aidan. "Look at them, they're huge."

"Which lorry did it fall off the back of?"

"Don't be like that, Bren. I bought it, all above board, from that jewellers in Market Street."

"Oh yeah?"

"I can show you the receipt, if you like."

"Where can you find the money to buy a ring like this?"

"Well, I just did, that's all."

"Not from roofing, I'm sure of that."

"Does it matter?"

"Yes, Aidan, it bloody does!"

Aidan paused for a moment, sulkily. "You know where I got the money," he said at last.

"Aidan!"

"We need a few treats, Bren! We can't just live skimping all the time."

"Not like this. Not unless you earned the money fair and square."

"Oh, I earned it all right! Don't you worry about that! I put my neck on the line—"

"I don't want you to," said Brenda desperately.

"So those posh bastards can take the biggest whack. But that's going to change, I've made up my mind."

"Don't do anything silly, Aidey. I just want you safe, so does Sharon. I don't want any silly ring."

"Put it on, love. It'll look beautiful on you."

"No," Brenda said decisively. "No, I don't want it." She put it down on the table.

"Bren!"

"You can just go and get your money back."

Aidan blew through his lips. "Can't do anything right, can I!"

"Not like this. No, you can't."

"But I love you," he said sincerely. "I want to show you how much I love you."

"You'll do that best by giving all this up, by not getting involved in stuff you can't handle."

"I can handle it all right," Aidan bridled. "I'm a match for those poxy stuck-ups any day."

Brenda looked at her husband steadily. "Give it up, Aidan."

He shifted from foot to foot. "I'm not sure I can. I'm not sure they'll let me."

"Bloody hell, Aidan!"

"It'll be all right."

"Will it?"

"I promise you."

"No, Aidan – don't promise me anything."

"But it will."

Brenda regarded him a little longer.

"You're a fool, Aidan Harvey," she said at length. "I love you too. It's a quarter past three, I'm going to pick up Sharon."

And she went out, leaving the ring on the table.

* * *

Wendy was undecided. She had none of her elder sister's desire for convention, none of her younger sister's impudence, none of her mother's restless ambition; she rather liked things to go on, just as they were, without any unsettling change.

But she'd met Philip, and she quite liked him, and, she thought, he quite liked her. They'd been on numerous dates together. Were their first get-togethers dates? She'd never really had a boyfriend before, just the odd hug and snog when she was still at school, and since then, nothing. Until Philip. Did sitting on a park bench eating your lunchtime sandwiches count as a date, before she went back to the office and he went back to the library? Going for a drink together after work definitely counted as a date, she decided.

They met first a year or so ago when she went to the library to return hers and her mother's books, and to pick out some new ones. He'd only just started there, and she felt a little lifting of her spirits when she saw this new face behind the counter, with its funny, happily puzzled expression. They'd talked a little longer than the mere transaction of the books demanded, about nothing very much, and after that Wendy found herself changing her library books more often than usual.

"Haven't you finished that book yet, Mum," she asked Jenny.

"You only took it out for me on Monday," her mother complained.

"Well, I've finished mine already."

"Then you go and change yours, and I'll keep mine a little longer."

"I was just asking, as I'm going anyway."

Their first meeting for lunch on the park bench was not quite a coincidence. Wendy had taken to spending her lunch hour in a café opposite the library, and one day, when she saw Philip come out for his midday break, she sort of followed him and sort of saw him sit on the bench and eat his sandwiches from a red-topped Tupperware box. So the next day she chose sandwiches over the café, and happened also to choose the very same bench as Philip's habitual bench on which to eat them. He smiled his happily puzzled smile when he found her there, and they chatted away easily.

This pleasant state of affairs continued for a month or so – several months in fact, for Philip was, Wendy judged, much like herself in his approbation of the status quo. But finally he stirred himself and suggested a drink after work, and Wendy found herself saying that it was a very nice idea. And it was: they spent a thoroughly amicable couple of hours together, before Wendy thought she'd better get home or her mother would be worried. More drinks after work followed, each one drifting a little longer into the evening, until Jenny couldn't help but notice something was up, though Wendy never told her anything about it.

Eventually Philip asked Wendy if she'd like to go to the cinema with him. Now that really *was* a date! She hesitated, the impulse to keep things as they were stalling the desire to say "yes", but the latter won the battle and they agreed to meet outside the cinema at seven the next evening. The film was enjoyable enough, as was, as usual, Philip's company. He offered to walk her home, which she allowed him to, though making him leave her at the end of the street, so her mother wouldn't see anything through her bedroom curtains. After the next cinema trip, he was so bold as to kiss her on the cheek as they parted on the street corner, and she found she liked it. A few trips later, the kiss was on the lips, and she found she really liked that.

But now he'd asked her to marry him, and she was undecided. She rather liked the current set-up: the pleasant company, the evenings out, the kiss at the end of the road, her life at home the same as it always had been. And if they got married, her mother would *have* to know about it. She wasn't quite sure why she didn't want Jenny to know she had a boyfriend; perhaps she was afraid deep down it would take the frisson out of her's and Philip's times together, make it ordinary. But on the other hand, what was all that semi-conscious engineering of their first lunch together on the park bench for, if not for this.

All that upheaval, though, all that fuss! Could she bear it? Maybe, she thought, and she did quite like him.

* * *

It was dark when Aidan met them; it always was. The time changed regularly, but it was never in daylight: sometimes, as on that first occasion, it was just before dawn, sometimes it was in the evening, sometimes in the middle of the night – he had trouble explaining those small hour absences to Brenda. Tonight it was 11 pm – Brenda would just assume he'd got drunk, and was staying with his mates at the Black Swan until they all got thrown out.

The location changed regularly too. Tonight they were in an ill-lit car park behind the station.

But the action was always the same. Aidan would hand over a wad of banknotes to the deep-voiced man with maybe a hint of a foreign accent, who would count it meticulously, nod and hand it to his companion, the man with the aristocratic accent, who would slip it into his inside left jacket pocket. Then the deep-voiced man with maybe a hint of a foreign accent would take an anonymous-looking package from his capacious coat pocket and hand it to Aidan, who would tuck it away under his zipped-up bomber jacket.

The man with the aristocratic accent never spoke. Neither, often, did the deep-voiced man with maybe a hint of a foreign accent. Maybe he'd lost his possible hint of a foreign accent; maybe the other had developed a Wiltshire burr.

The transaction done, the two men turned on their heels and left as abruptly as they'd arrived. Aidan took a half bottle of whisky out of his pocket and had a swig, just so Brenda would smell the alcohol on his breath.

* * *

Pretend "Uncle" Arthur sat on the sofa in Jenny's front room, nursing a cup and saucer; Jenny sat in her usual armchair; William was in the kitchen, performing his habitual and not unwelcome task of washing up after lunch.

"We don't seem to see so much of you as we used to, Arthur," Jenny said.

"No, well…" Arthur smiled a little awkwardly and pushed the spectacles back up his nose. "It's good to see you've got someone to support you, Jenny."

"Support me?"

"Well, you know…"

"I'm quite capable of supporting myself, thank you very much. I have a very good income from my investments."

"Yes."

"The money from the little job I had was just for fun."

"That's not what I meant. You know it isn't." Jenny didn't say anything, so Arthur went on, "Everyone should have someone to be there for them, if ever they need it."

"You've always been there for me, Arthur."

"I'm glad." He paused a moment. "And I'm glad you and William get on so well too."

"There's nothing going on like that, you know."

Arthur smiled again. "I never suggested there was. But it's nice to see you have a close friend."

They sat in comfortable silence for a minute or so.

"Do you miss your little job?" Arthur asked, genuinely interested.

"No," said Jenny, and then, "yes. It was pleasant to have somewhere I had to go, and to meet people other than friends and family."

"I can imagine."

"But apart from that…" She trailed off.

"How *are* the family?"

"Oh…" She hesitated before going on. "Robert and Maria seem happy enough in their tiny house in Bromley."

"A new baby, I understand."

"Yes. Christine. They brought her down to see me."

"A grandmother again."

"Yes. *They* can look forward to all the squabbles and bother now."

"You think they'll have more?"

"Oh yes. That seems to be the life Robert's chosen for himself."

"He's happy, though?"

"Yes. Very."

"How are Susan's two?"

"Very neat, very clever apparently."

"Really!"

"Philippa starts high school this autumn."

"It hardly seems possible."

"High school!" said Jenny derogatorily. "I'm sure I don't know what was wrong with the grammar school system."

"No. Perhaps." Arthur had a sip of tea. "And Sharon?"

"Oh, she's a real bright spark!" Jenny's eyes lit up. "Like her mother, but without the surliness."

"I've never thought of Brenda as surly."

"You didn't bring her up."

"Just forthright, I'd say."

"Very. Though sometimes, when she's with that man…" She left the sentence unfinished.

A pause.

"They muddle along, I expect," said Arthur ineffectually.

"'Muddle' being the operative word."

"If ever you need any help from me."

"Thank you, Arthur. But I think I'm more than a match for Aidan Harvey." She sat for a moment, lost in thought. "I do worry about Brenda, though," she said at last.

Before Arthur could add anything, William popped his head round the door.

"Anyone for a top-up?" he asked.

"That would be lovely, William," said Arthur.

London

"Ah! What a beauty!" Thomas exclaimed.

"She's lovely," said Hazel.

"And so pretty," András added.

Maria and Robert had taken baby Christine round to meet them all at the Kensington flat.

"May I hold her?" asked Thomas, holding out his hands.

"Of course, Uncle," said Maria, lifting Christine out of her pram and handing her to him.

"My little great-niece," Thomas cooed, lifting her high in the air.

"Careful, Thomas," Robert warned.

"He's fine," reassured his wife.

"Of course I'm fine!" said Thomas jovially. "I held her mother like this when she was the same age."

"Did you?" asked Maria.

"Certainly I did. You were two years old before all that nonsense started up, and András and I had to come here."

"That's right, I was."

Robert looked on, a proud father. It felt like no time at all since he had lived in this flat himself; and yet it seemed like a lifetime away. How things turned out! All those little links in the chain! A single one missed could have mapped out an entirely different future for him: his mother wanting him to be an actor, going to RADA, going to Thomas for photos, meeting Maria in Budapest. As he watched the little scene playing out in front of him, he realised he wouldn't have wished it any other way.

"Would you like to hold her, Hazel?" Maria asked.

"Oh! Yes please. If I may."

"Of course you may," said Thomas, swooping baby Christine down into her arms.

Hazel sat holding the baby on her lap, slightly awkwardly, but very happy.

"And so we must celebrate!" declared Thomas, a familiar theme.

"No, Uncle, no!" said Maria, decisively but kindly. "A cup of tea will be quite sufficient."

"Suit yourselves," Thomas said, a little grumpily.

"I'll put the kettle on," said András, with a smile.

SIXTEEN

1983

TROWBRIDGE

Aidan handed over the money and the other counted it, but this time he didn't hand it straight on to his companion. He looked up at Aidan for a moment, and then back to the wad of money to count it again. Eventually he turned to his companion with a vaguely quizzical look, finally nodded, and handed him the money, which the latter pocketed in the habitual way.

"Everything all right, I hope," ventured Aidan.

"So do I," said the first man. His voice was still deep, and with maybe a hint of a foreign accent.

He drew the expected anonymous-looking package from his pocket and handed it to Aidan, and then, as usual, with no more ado, the two men turned away and left. Aidan looked down at the unmarked brown envelope. That had all happened as it always did, and yet somehow this time he felt uneasy. Well, even more than he normally did. He shook his mane of shaggy dark hair to dismiss his misgivings, and went back to the van.

* * *

Back at home, Aidan poured himself a whisky and looked at the clock – 2 am. He'd let himself into the house very quietly, and hadn't woken Brenda. Or, at least, he thought he hadn't. He'd tell her he'd gone back to a mate's house for a game of poker, a spur of the moment thing. She'd probably believe him.

He sat down at the dining table in the back room and took another wad of notes out of his pocket, not as thick as the wad he'd handed over half an hour ago, but still substantial enough. He counted it, paused for a moment thinking, and then counted it again.

"Shit!" he said to himself, under his breath. "I miscounted. I gave them too much."

BUDAPEST

"She does not think of me," said Irina robustly.

"She thinks of you a lot," countered János. "She's just spent all her holiday with you."

"She spent two weeks with me."

"That is all her holiday."

"Her husband's holiday."

"Her husband's, yes. It's the same thing."

"I do not think so."

"I do," said János, matching his wife's firmness. "They're married, he works, his holiday is her holiday."

Irina held her counsel for a moment or two and then tried a different tack.

"He did not think it through, when he turned her head and took her away. He did not consider all the consequences."

"They fell in love, my darling," said János, softening. "Like you and I fell in love. Don't you remember?"

"You didn't take me away from my family. You didn't take me to another country."

"I didn't need to. We both lived here in Budapest."

"That's what I mean."

"Besides, it wasn't just Robert's doing. He couldn't have made Maria marry him if she didn't want to. She takes after you. She's a headstrong girl."

"I'm not headstrong."

"You are. Listen to yourself now." He gathered his thoughts. "I tell you, Maria knows her own mind, and she made up her mind, and she married Robert. And now they have a child, a lovely little daughter."

"Whose childhood I will miss."

"No you won't. They will think of you, of both of us, include us. They'll send photos, visit as often as they can. Robert is a good man, a kind man. He will make sure we're not left out."

Irina's unyielding facade slipped a little. "But I miss her," she said passionately. "I miss her so much."

János took her in his arms. "I know you do, my dear. So do I. Let me hug you."

And they stood, holding each other tight, for several minutes, until Irina broke away a little and said, "It's all your brother's fault, as usual. Whatever did Tamás think he was doing, sending that boy over here in the first place!"

TROWBRIDGE

Sharon was sat at Jenny's kitchen table with her mum

and nana, though she wasn't taking any notice of them apparently; all her attention seemed to be focussed on the drawing in front of her, as she made it more and more elaborate, adding this touch here and that touch there, and choosing her colours carefully from the array of felt-tip pens spread out on the table around the sheet of paper she was working on. She used to like colouring books, but now she preferred inventing her own pictures out of her imagination. Today's was of a unicorn, flying past a princess in a castle. It was really very good.

Jenny watched her granddaughter proudly; Brenda was lost in her own thoughts. It had become a comfortable habit, Brenda and Sharon dropping in to see Jenny on their way home from school – well, not really on the way, but not a massive detour – before getting home for tea and Sharon's dad, if he turned up. Sometimes they stayed at Jenny's for tea, but Aidan didn't really like that.

"A penny for them," said Jenny, looking at her daughter.

"Mm?" murmured Brenda, coming back from far away.

"Are you all right, dear?"

"Yes. Of course I am."

"Are you? Really?"

Brenda tried to stop this interrogation. "Mum!" she said meaningfully, nodding towards her absorbed daughter.

"Oh," Jenny said, "don't worry about Sharon. She's not taking any notice of us. Are you, dear?"

"Don't you believe it!"

Sharon said nothing, but just sucked the top of her felt-tip pen thoughtfully, before adding another self-assured line.

"Well?" said Jenny, not to be put off.

"Well, it's difficult, isn't it."

"I should think so! All that ridiculous business last year!"

"I've said sorry about that."

"It's not your business to say sorry; that's someone else's business entirely."

"He'll never say sorry."

"I know he won't. He'll never admit he's wrong about anything. That's part of the difficulty, I imagine."

Brenda looked at her mother. "You think I made a huge mistake, don't you?" she said.

Jenny didn't answer immediately. "Are you happy, Brenda?" she asked at last.

Brenda didn't answer immediately either. Eventually, "I love him, Mum," she said simply.

"That's not the same thing at all. Believe me – I know." Jenny watched as Sharon shaded the cloud she'd just added to her picture, and then said to Brenda, "I only want everything to be all right for you, as it is for Susan and Robert."

"Oh, I'm just as good as them, don't you worry," Brenda said sharply, her hackles rising.

"I never said you weren't."

"No? Well, it sounded like it."

"Nothing could be further from my mind."

"And what about Wendy, anyway?" Brenda asked, trying to call a halt to the therapy session. "Has she still got her boyfriend?"

"Wendy's fine."

"Philip, is it?"

"So I believe."

"Do you think they'll get married?"

"I'll be surprised if they get around to anything. I've never come across such a pair of dawdlers."

"I hope they do get married. Sharon would make a lovely bridesmaid."

"Don't want to be a bridesmaid," said Sharon forcibly, speaking for the first time in a good long while.

Bristol

"There has been a complaint."

The voice was deep and if anything the hint of a foreign accent was a little more pronounced than usual. He spoke as soon as they were both in the car and the doors were shut.

"A complaint?" The aristocratic accent was unmistakable, although the words were spoken softly and calmly. "What sort of a complaint? From whom?"

"A customer."

"You have nothing to do with customers."

"I know."

"Did one of the runners pass it on?"

"No. The complaint was overheard."

"Overheard?"

"Yes."

"Where?"

"In a pub. Two men talking. None of our people involved at all. But word gets back to me."

"What was said?"

"Someone who'd bought recently, complaining to his friend that the stuff wasn't pure, something else cut in with it."

"That's not good. How do you know it came from one of ours?"

"The person complaining named the runner."

"Ah." The owner of the aristocratic voice hesitated briefly. "Do you know it? This name?"

"Yes."

The apparent aristocrat thought for a moment, and then said, "Everything we supply is a hundred per cent pure, isn't it."

"Yes," replied the foreign-voiced gentleman.

"Isn't it!" repeated the other forcefully, demanding definite confirmation.

"Yes!" affirmed his informant, maybe sounding the slightest bit unsettled for the first time in the conversation.

"Well, we must deal with that, mustn't we."

"Yes."

"I don't like people trying to pull a fast one on me."

"No."

"You know what to do?"

The briefest of pauses, and then, "Yes."

No further exchange. The foreign-voiced gentleman turned the key in the ignition and the car purred into life. He touched the accelerator and they pulled out of the private drive and turned towards the M4.

SEVENTEEN

Trowbridge

A discreet tap brought Brenda to the front door. Sergeant Hopkins stood on the doorstep, the same policeman who'd visited her and Aidan after the incident at Thomas's London flat. It was a Saturday morning and she'd been doing some housework – she still had the duster in her hand; Sharon was upstairs in her room, drawing as usual. Something about the officer's kindly expression made her blood run cold; usually there was a cheerful insistence about his manner when he called round, but today he was entirely different.

"Good morning, Mrs Harvey," he said and, "Brenda," he added gently. "May I come in please?"

She'd been expecting something. Aidan hadn't come home last night; that wasn't unprecedented, but usually he'd turned up by 11 am, or at least phoned to offer his explanation, which she either chose to believe or not. The housework had been a distraction, to stop her thinking about what accident or beating-up might have befallen him.

When they were sat in the front room, Sergeant Hopkins began compassionately, but with practised ease, "I'm terribly sorry, Brenda, but I've got some bad news."

"Oh my God!" said Brenda, blanching, and now, suddenly, fearing the worst, which it was.

Aidan's body had been found in the woods where he first met the drug suppliers. Two joggers had caught sight of it, spread-eagled behind a bush beside their habitual path. He'd been stabbed with a kitchen knife, and had been there for several hours, the police thought. For all intents and purposes, they considered this to be a murder inquiry.

Brenda just stared, blankly, numbed, unable to react. "What am I going to tell Sharon?" she said at last.

"Where is she now?" asked the sergeant softly.

"Upstairs, in her room," she said automatically.

"Good. Shall I put on the kettle?" he offered, "or can I pour you something a little stronger?"

"No. I don't want anything." She still couldn't work out what to feel.

"I shall need to ask you just a few questions, you see," explained Hopkins. "I really think perhaps a cup of tea—"

"All right," Brenda conceded. "Tea. Please," she added.

"You stay here, eh? I won't be a moment."

The policeman went into the kitchen and deftly made two mugs of tea, effortlessly finding everything he needed at the first or second attempt.

"Would you like sugar?" he asked when he came back with the two mugs, a teaspoon and a packet of sugar on a round plastic tray.

"Yes, please. Two."

He spooned in two for her, one for himself, stirred both, handed her hers, and sat down again with his.

"When did you last see Aidan?" he asked, after he'd taken his first sip.

"Last night, about ten o'clock." Her tea remained untasted.

"Do you know where he was going?"

"He said he was going to the pub."

"I see." Sergeant Hopkins took another sip, and then went on, "Do you think he was?"

Brenda paused for a moment before she said, "Maybe."

"Where else might he have gone?"

Brenda shrugged. "Who knows?"

"Not you?"

"Last person."

Another sip for the policeman. "Did he often lie to you – about where he was going, I mean?"

"Sometimes," she replied sullenly.

"But you don't know where he went instead?"

"No."

"Do you know what he might have been doing, wherever he was?"

Brenda didn't answer, but took her first sip of tea.

"Brenda?" Hopkins encouraged.

"He was getting into something silly, I think," she said uninformatively.

"Oh yes? What sort of something silly?" and then, when Brenda remained silent, "Something illegal?"

"I think," Brenda acknowledged, but added nothing.

"Drugs?" the sergeant continued to coax. "Dealing drugs, I mean?" He felt like he was pulling teeth.

"I think," she repeated.

"How long for, do you know?"

"A few months." The sergeant looked at her quizzically. "A year or so, maybe," she added.

"I see." Hopkins cradled his mug, and then held it by the handle again. "Did he ever talk to you about it?"

"He did it for us," said Brenda, opening up a little.

"For you?"

"For me and Sharon."

"Oh?"

"He wanted us to live better. He was embarrassed when we couldn't afford things."

"And so he started dealing drugs."

"I told him not to. I told him we didn't care. We just wanted him safe and well." And then she cried. She cried long, and loud, and uncontrollably. Sergeant Hopkins took her mug from her, but she didn't notice. A moment later Sharon appeared at the hall door.

"Mummy!" she said, upset. "What's the matter?"

She went to her mother and Brenda hugged her tightly, still sobbing.

"Mummy!" Sharon tried again, starting to cry herself.

Hopkins sat silently watching them for a few moments, but then, as Brenda's convulsions subsided a little, he ventured, "Sharon?"

"Who are you?" asked the little girl between sobs.

"My name's Dave," the sergeant said. "Dave Hopkins, and I'm a policeman." Sharon looked scared and hugged her mother closer. "Your mum's got some sad news to tell you."

And then Brenda told her, simply, that "Daddy was dead", and Sharon cried again, and Brenda cried with her, and then, before Sharon could ask any more questions, Brenda said, "I must ring Mum."

* * *

Brenda's phone call, and the information it imparted, was not really a surprise to Jenny. She knew, or thought she knew, her son-in-law better than anyone, perhaps even better than Brenda knew him herself. For years she'd suspected the kind of underworld he moved in, the kind of people he associated with, dealt with, the kind of illegality in which he was involved. She had felt so anxious for her daughter, and latterly for her granddaughter, and yet so helpless, unable to make any amends, and she knew her fractious relationship with Aidan, the constant bickering and intermittent flare-up arguments, only made things worse for Brenda. But somehow she couldn't help herself. When the news came through of an outcome Jenny had long thought might be inevitable, in some ways she felt a sense of relief; but she felt – oh, how she felt! – such love and sympathy and care for her daughter.

"Shall I come round, darling?" she asked Brenda.

"Yes please, Mum. Please."

"I'll call William."

"No!" Brenda was suddenly adamant. "No William. Please."

"All right, darling. If you don't want him there."

"I don't."

"He could just drop me off?"

"No. Can you ring for a taxi?"

"Yes. All right." Jenny waited a moment, and then added, "I love you, darling."

"I love you too, Mum. Come quickly. Please."

"I will. Goodbye, darling."

Brenda hung up before Jenny, and without another word. Jenny didn't replace the handset but rattled the cradle a couple of times to get a fresh dialling tone, and then dialled the number on the taxi business card which she kept beside the phone. By the time the taxi arrived ten minutes later, she had her coat and scarf on and was ready to go.

Bromley

The phone rang about half-past six on Monday evening. Robert answered it; he had just arrived home from work.

"They think I am a murderer," said the Hungarian accented voice at the other end of the line.

"What?" said Robert, trying to catch up. "Thomas. What's happened?"

"The police. They think I am a murderer."

"What? Why? Surely not."

"They came to visit me this afternoon. They said, 'Where were you on Friday evening? Where were you on Saturday morning?' I said, 'I was at home, here, in my flat.' They said, 'Can you prove this?' I said, 'How do I prove it?' They said, 'Was anyone here with you?' I said, 'No. András my friend was at work on a full weekend shift. Hazel my friend was away for the weekend visiting her parents.' They said, 'That's awkward.' I said, 'Why awkward?' They said, 'It would've been helpful to have some corroboration rather than just your say so.'." Thomas ended this rapid summation of his interview with the police by adding, "They think I am a murderer."

"I don't understand. Why did they visit you?"

"They think, because your brother-in-law threatened to kill me, I get in first."

"Aidan!"

"They think I go all the way to Trowbridge on Friday night and stab him with a knife."

"But that's ridiculous."

"Of course it is ridiculous! I told them, 'This is ridiculous!' They said, 'Murder isn't ridiculous, sir,' and then they explained to me the whole story."

Robert already knew the story. His mother had phoned him on Saturday afternoon to tell him what had happened, and he'd driven to Trowbridge on Sunday to see Brenda and Sharon; Maria had stayed at home in Bromley with Christine. Brenda hadn't talked to him much. She was still in a state of shock, and not quite reacting to anyone properly. Sharon hugged her uncle for fully five minutes and cried. Robert didn't really know what to do. He wasn't sure his visit had done any good, but at least he'd been there, he supposed.

Jenny seemed to have come into her own. She'd taken control of the situation and Brenda didn't show any signs of objecting; her flat refusal to have anything to do with William was the only indication she had any strong opinions on the subject. In spite of this, and without Brenda's knowledge, Jenny had telephoned William and asked him to do some shopping for them, which he duly did, leaving it discreetly outside the front gate for Jenny to collect. Jenny had cooked tea for herself, Brenda and Sharon on Saturday evening, and stopped over, sleeping on the sofa; then a full roast lunch for Robert as well the day after. Wendy, Susan and her husband Peter had also come round on Sunday morning, but they didn't stay to lunch. They each said if there was anything they could do…

Robert left to drive back to Bromley just after four, but Jenny stayed the night again – Sharon said she'd like her to.

It had been decided over Sunday lunch that Sharon shouldn't go to school on Monday morning. Jenny phoned the school first thing the next day and explained the situation, and the headmaster and her teacher were both shocked, but then very understanding; perhaps in a few days.

"What's happened now?" asked Maria, coming down the stairs from settling Christine and reading her a bedtime story.

"It's Uncle Thomas," said Robert, still on the phone. "The police have come to see him about Aidan."

"What? Here, let me talk to him. You go and kiss Christine goodnight."

Robert handed the receiver to Maria and went up the stairs.

TROWBRIDGE

Detective Inspector Turner perched on the edge of his desk and dug his hands deep into his pockets.

"What time are we meeting her?" he asked his colleague.

"Eleven o'clock at the morgue," replied Detective Sergeant Ferris, sat at another desk alongside. "Her mother's coming with her. She says her daughter's up to it now."

"Whether she is or not, she's got to do it. And then we'll have a talk with her."

"Hopkins seems to think there's a drug connection. Apparently she admitted as much when he spoke to her on Saturday."

"It looks likely, I guess. Anything from London, with that foreign bloke? The one Harvey threatened?"

"Says he was at home all the time, apparently. But there's no-one to back up his story."

"Does he drive?"

"They didn't say."

"Find out, will you?"

"Right."

"And then go through all the usual druggies – dealers and customers, everyone we have a record of or know of otherwise – see if they can account for themselves Friday night Saturday morning."

"Yes, sir."

The identification of the body was fairly routine. The morgue attendant lifted the sheet and Brenda looked at the face of her dead husband. She didn't show any emotion, just stared at it for a moment or two before nodding, almost imperceptibly. DI Turner and DS Ferris stood a few steps back; Jenny was even further off, by the door.

"Yes?" Turner prompted, wanting verbal backup to the nod.

"Yes," said Brenda, huskily.

"Thank you, Mrs Harvey. Shall we?" The detective inspector gestured towards the door and the attendant replaced the sheet over Aidan's face.

Once they were in the hall, Turner went on, "Perhaps you wouldn't mind coming back to the station with Sergeant Ferris and myself now. We can have a cup of tea and go through a few things."

"Everyone wants to give me tea," said Brenda.

"Or we have coffee," Turner offered.

Brenda looked at him. "I told Sergeant Hopkins all I know on Saturday morning."

"Nevertheless," said Turner with a little smile.

"Go with them, Brenda," said Jenny. "It's for the best."

"I don't think I have a choice, Mum. Do I?" she asked, turning to the inspector.

Turner smiled again and gave a little shake of his head. "Not really," he said. "But we could come round to yours, if you need to get back – for your little girl, I mean."

"Sharon's with my sister," said Brenda.

"Susan will be in no rush," confirmed Jenny. "I'll come with you, darling. I mean, if that's permitted?" she added to the inspector.

"That's fine, Mrs Markham," Turner confirmed. "You can wait in the next room while we talk to Mrs Harvey."

"This must be cleared up," Jenny said.

Half an hour later Turner was back perched on his desk, with Ferris sat at his desk alongside, and Brenda sat in front of them; Jenny was next door with a cup of the ubiquitous tea.

Brenda went over again what she'd already told Sergeant Hopkins – how Aidan had said he was going to the pub, how he sometimes stayed out all night without explanation, how she thought he might have been dealing drugs for several years, she wasn't sure, how she'd begged him to stop. It was good for them to hear it for themselves.

"But he didn't stop?" Turner pursued.

Brenda shook her head. "I think he wanted to," she added.

"You mean he'd got himself into something he couldn't get out of?" Turner asked.

"Something like."

"Cannabis?"

Sharon shrugged.

"Cocaine? Hard drugs?"

"Yeah. I think."

"Did you ever see anything about the house?"

"No. Not really."

"Not really?"

"A bit of powder left on the table now and then, if he hadn't cleaned up. I told him don't you dare leave anything lying around – because of Sharon."

"White powder?"

"Mm."

"Heroin?"

"I wouldn't know."

"No?"

"No."

"But he was bagging it himself?"

Brenda shrugged again, and Turner made a note on a sheet of paper beside him.

"Did he ever mention any names to you?" he asked, looking up again.

"No."

"Who he bought from? Who he sold to?"

"I tell you he never spoke to me about it! I've told you all I know. Honestly. He wanted to protect me and Sharon."

"Hm!" Turner muttered, standing up, as if to say, "Funny way of going about it!" though he didn't vocalise the sentiment.

"No-one ever came to the house?" he asked, going over to look out of the first-floor window.

"Not that I ever saw."

"You never went through his pockets, to try and find out more about what he was up to?"

"No!"

"Honestly?"

"I didn't want to know anything about it."

Turner tried another tack: "Did he ever take the drugs himself, I wonder?"

Brenda shifted in her seat. "Not that I ever saw."

"Did you?"

"No!"

"Never?"

"A bit of pot, that's all. Years ago, long before all this started."

The inspector turned back from the window. "How was Aidan recently?"

"What do you mean how was he?"

"Well, was he as he normally was? Did he seem more agitated than usual? More jumpy?"

"A bit, maybe." Brenda thought for a moment and then said, "But he was sad, more than anything. Yeah. He seemed sad lately." She stared ahead of her, not seeing anything. "So sad."

The inspector and the sergeant exchanged glances.

"Thank you, Mrs Harvey," said Turner. "I'll get a car to run you and Mrs Markham home."

* * *

Sharon leapt out of the car.

"Nana!" she cried, and ran up the garden path to hug Jenny, who hugged her back.

"There you are, Sharon," she said. "Have you had a nice time with Auntie Susan?"

She felt the girl nod against her as they hugged.

"We made cakes, didn't we, Sharon?" said Susan, standing at the gate. "And then lots of drawing, of course."

"Drawing is good," said Jenny. "As much drawing as you like. Brenda's in the bathroom," she said to Susan. "Will you come in and say 'hello'?"

"I'd better get back, Mum, if you don't mind. Peter's on call tonight so I promised him an early meal."

"As you wish," said Jenny. "Thank you for having Sharon."

"It was a pleasure. It's always a pleasure. She's a lovely girl, and Philippa and James love seeing her."

"She *is* a lovely girl," Jenny repeated, hugging Sharon closer.

"Let me know if you need me to help again," said Susan, getting back into her car. "Bye."

"I will, darling," returned Jenny. "Goodbye."

Susan pulled the car door shut and started the engine. Jenny and Sharon stood on the doorstep to wave her off and then went into the house, just as Brenda was hurrying down the stairs.

"Mum!" Sharon ran to her.

"Darling." She hugged Sharon tight, and they stood together, holding each other, for several minutes. Jenny left them alone and went into the kitchen. She put the kettle on the stove and lit the gas.

* * *

"There's any number of possibles," said Inspector Turner to his superior, "but no obvious definites. At least, none we can pin down."

"Nasty business," acknowledged Superintendent Marshall, sitting behind the desk in his office. "Be good to clear it up as soon as possible."

"That's what the mother said."

"Mm?"

"Aidan Harvey's mother-in-law. She said this must be cleared up."

"Well she's right, isn't she! That's our job."

"Yes, sir."

"Worth pulling any of the possibles in, do you think? Pushing it a bit further?"

"Ferris and I, we'll go through everything again this afternoon, see if anything jumps out."

"And get our chaps out there amongst them. Be on show. Make them edgy. Someone may give something away."

"Yes, sir."

"Good to be on show."

"Yes, sir."

Back with Sergeant Ferris, Turner was philosophical. "I thought I'd have fun, being a policeman," he said.

"Fun, sir?"

"Dashing about, solving cases, gathering all the suspects together and making the big reveal."

"That's Agatha Christie, isn't it, sir?"

"If you like."

"I've read one or two of them. I prefer *James Bond*, if I'm honest."

"You surprise me!" Turner said wryly, and then added gloomily, "It's not glamorous at all, is it?"

"Tell me about it, sir!"

"Mostly it's just boring routine – and very nasty."

"Horrible," Ferris agreed, and twirled the wedding ring on his finger, longing for five o'clock and time to go home. All being well.

Bristol

"A knife is good," said the man with the aristocratic accent, having shaken his associate's hand. "It conveys a hint of the Italian, the Mafia, a touch of revenge."

"Just so," said the deep-voiced man with maybe a hint of a foreign accent.

"An appropriate warning to anyone else who might think of starting out on their own, against us," the other continued.

"I agree," said his subordinate, "but it wasn't me."

"No. Of course. One of your contacts."

"Not even that."

"No?" The aristocratic-voiced man raised his eyebrows quizzically.

"I had set things in motion, made all the arrangements."

"As we agreed."

"But he was dead before we had a chance to act. Someone had already killed him."

The aristocratic man thought for a moment. "Curious," he said, and then added, "Ah well, it's saved us a job."

"Yes."

"Safer, too. Let the others think it was us, if they choose to – the warning is still the same."

"Yes."

"Do you think he was moonlighting, working for anyone else?"

"It's possible."

"That might explain it. If so, they've done us a favour."

"The police have started sniffing around."

"They know it's drugs then."

"It seems."

"We'll call a halt to things for a while, a few months, keep a low profile."

It was the turn of the deep-voiced man with maybe a hint of a foreign accent to raise his eyebrows quizzically. "We do keep a low profile," he said.

"You know what I mean," said the other, a disagreeable edge to his voice. "We've got a good set-up here. It would be foolish to spoil it."

Trowbridge

"Can I do anything to help?" asked "Uncle" Arthur at the other end of the line.

"I don't think so," replied Jenny, "though thank you for offering. I'm not staying over anymore. Brenda seems a little more self-sufficient now."

"Good."

"It's not a bad idea for her and Sharon to have some time to themselves, I think – work things through together."

"Just *be* together, maybe."

"Exactly."

"Is Sharon back at school yet?"

"Starting again next Monday."

"I hope she gets on all right. Other children can be very cruel."

"The staff know all about it, so they can keep an eye on things."

"Good."

"I think she's going to be fine."

"That's good."

Both were silent for a moment, and then Arthur asked, "The police are no closer to finding out who did it?"

"No. I understand they think it could be something to do with drugs."

"Shocking!"

"Aidan was involved somehow, I believe, though I don't think Brenda knew anything about it."

"You must've been so worried."

"I was."

Arthur went on tentatively, "It's an awful thing to say, but in some ways, you know, this may all be for the best."

Jenny considered the idea, not for the first time. "I don't think Brenda thinks like that," she said at last, "however true it may be."

"No. Of course not," said Arthur.

EIGHTEEN

1984

KENSINGTON

It was a grand reunion meal. Thomas was hosting, with András and Hazel in attendance. Robert had driven himself, Maria and Christine over to the Kensington flat, having arrived home from work a little earlier. The little toddler enjoyed running around the living room, exploring new things.

"It will be late, of course," Maria had protested.

"It won't hurt, once in a while," Robert had replied. "She'll enjoy meeting her uncles, and Auntie Hazel will love to see her. We can put her to sleep in her pushchair, and then I can carry her down to the car. She probably won't even wake up."

"It will unsettle her."

"Not really. And it will mean a lot to Thomas."

Reluctantly his wife acquiesced.

The atmosphere, as always at Thomas's soirées, was convivial; the food, all prepared by the host himself, was excellent, and of course the wine and pálinka flowed generously.

"You must let us wash up for you," said Maria, as Thomas started to clear the table.

"*Nem, nem!*" Thomas said firmly. "I shall do it later. I insist."

But Hazel knew in fact that she and András would do it, when the others had left, and when Thomas was asleep in his chair.

Once Christine had been settled in her pushchair in the spare room, and they were all sitting comfortably with refilled glasses of palinka – all except Maria, who chose coffee, made by András, over a refill – the conversation turned inevitably to the previous year's events in Trowbridge.

"Did the police ever visit you again?" asked Robert.

"They wanted to know if I could drive."

"Drive?"

"'No!' I told them. 'I do not need to drive. I have all I need here in London. I can walk to my studio, or to the shop, or to the pub. Or I can take the Tube. Why do I need to drive?' But they do not believe me. They checked with their records to see if I have a driving licence. They told me."

"It's their job," said András. "Of course they will check up."

"But they didn't come back after that?" pursued Robert.

"*Nem.* No. But I expect them at any moment."

"Oh, I'm sure they've discounted you now, Uncle," said Maria. "So long after, and you couldn't possibly have anything to do with it."

"It is all because of that stupid nonsense with your brother-in-law, Robert. They think I have a motive."

"That was years ago now," said Maria. "Surely not."

"We shall see," said Thomas, unconvinced.

"But haven't they got any further with it?" asked Hazel, who was fully up-to-date with a thoroughly embellished version of the murder, as furnished to her by Thomas.

"Not as far as I know," said Robert. "My mother keeps tabs on the progress, in so far as she can, and she's told me nothing new recently. They still think it's drugs, but they've just come up against a lot of brick walls, apparently."

"And how is your sister?" András asked Robert. "It must be horrible for her and your niece."

"Brenda wants nothing to do with it," Robert said. "If ever the subject's raised, she shuts it down immediately. I called her the other day, and when I touched on it she just started talking about my mother's friend William. She didn't even acknowledge I'd mentioned it."

"I suppose that's natural," said Hazel.

"It will be for the best," said András.

"The sooner it's forgotten, the better," observed Maria.

"One day soon, they will arrest me," said Thomas gloomily.

"Nonsense, Uncle," said Maria.

"Come!" said the elder Hungarian, snapping out of his sombre mood. "More pálinka! Robert?"

"No. Best not," Robert said reluctantly. "I've got to drive home in a while. I wouldn't mind a coffee, if you don't mind?"

"One coffee coming up," András said, jumping up. "Another for you, Maria?"

"Yes, please."

"Pálinka for you, András?" Thomas called after him.

"You haven't got work tomorrow. And you, Hazel," he said, refilling her glass, "I know you'll have some more."

"Thank you, Thomas," Hazel said gratefully.

Trowbridge

It was raining. It had been raining all day. The drops chased down the office window as Turner looked out across the puddled car park. He turned back as Ferris entered the room.

"Anything?" he asked.

Ferris shook his head. "Away on the Costa del Sol at the time," he said. "Wife and kids to back him up."

"Wife and kids?" asked Turner suspiciously.

"And the hotel owner as well, I'm afraid. Our Spanish friends showed him the photo and he identified him immediately. And showed them his signature in the hotel register."

"Damn!"

"I know. All confirmed by the airline, too."

"Seems cut and dried, then."

"I'm afraid so."

"Well, that's it then, I suppose. Forensics, nothing. Narcotics, nothing. Leads from contacts and records, nothing. Hunches, nothing. We've got nowhere in over a year, and we've exhausted every avenue we can possibly think of. We'll have to put it on the back-burner."

"Close it down? Leave it unsolved?"

"No. Just leave it open. Something may land in our lap, but the super wants us on other things. Says he can't spare us any longer."

"Fair enough."

"For my money, Aidan Harvey was diluting the gear, making it go further, earning himself a bit extra on top. The high-ups found out about it and weren't best pleased, took their little revenge. Wanted to set an example, even. But I can't prove anything. We've drawn a blank on whoever was supplying him, so it's all just speculation."

Ferris let his superior's theory hang in the air for a few moments, and then said, "Shall I tell the family?"

"Eh? Oh, no. Like I said, it's just a theory."

"No. I mean that we're mothballing the case."

"Oh. No. I don't think so," said Turner thoughtfully. "No need to bother them. They can think we're still working on it. Well, we are in a way. As I say, it's still open. We're just awaiting developments."

* * *

William arrived at Jenny's front door just as Wendy was letting herself out.

"Oh. Sorry, William," Wendy said, seeing him coming up the path. "Mum's not in at the moment."

"Oh. Isn't she?" William was a little knocked off kilter. "That's funny. I usually pop round on a Tuesday. Take her out to lunch."

"Do you?"

"Yes. You don't know where she is, I suppose?"

"Afraid not. She didn't tell me."

"Ah. I see."

"Sorry."

"So you won't know when she's back, then."

"No. Sorry."

"My fault. I should've telephoned first."

"Possibly."

"It's just that we always…" William trailed off.

Wendy smiled at him. "I'm sure she'll call you later on," she offered by way of compensation. "Perhaps you can come round for tea."

"Yes. Perhaps." William seemed reluctant to go. "Not at work today?" he asked, changing the subject.

"No, I've taken a few days off."

"That's nice."

"Felt I deserved it."

"I'm sure. It's been quite a time for you all, hasn't it."

"A bit, yes."

"Are you doing anything nice while you're off?"

"Oh. No, not really."

"Are you and – er…" he paused. "Philip, is it?"

"Oh. No." Wendy looked away. "Philip and I – we're – well…"

"Oh?"

"We're not really seeing much of each other any more."

"Oh. I'm sorry."

"No. It's fine. It was me, really. It all became a bit too much for me. A bit too full on…"

"Ah."

"If you know what I mean."

"Well…" William returned the compliment with a gentle, sympathetic smile, "so long as you're happy, eh?"

"Oh, yes. I am. I…" Wendy started to offer an explanation, but then didn't really want to go on.

They both stood, indecisively, saying nothing.

"Well! Nice to see you, William," Wendy said at last.

"Yes."

"See you again soon, I hope."

"Yes. Oh, er – can I offer you a lift anywhere?"

"Oh, no thank you. I'd prefer to walk."

"Right. Fine. Goodbye then."

"Goodbye, William."

Outside Bath

The Mercedes-Benz turned off the lane and purred almost silently up the gravel drive. He parked as close as he could to the hotel entrance, turned off the engine with a satisfyingly minimal click of his ignition key, and then went round to open the passenger door for his guest.

"Very smart," said Jenny, as he helped her out of the car. "Five star?"

"Of course."

"Thank you for meeting me at the station."

"My pleasure."

"It seemed most discreet. Better than a taxi. They might remember me."

"I agree. Shall we?" He offered Jenny his arm, which she took, and they went in, through the foyer, to the dining room. They were greeted by the maître d', who conducted them to a table for two tucked away in an alcove.

"I chose this table especially," he said, once they were seated and the maître d' had left them alone, "so we can talk freely."

"You've done well," Jenny congratulated him. "I thought of afternoon tea at first—"

"Tiffin!" he said, and they both smiled.

"Exactly! But then, the idea of sitting in a foyer, or a lounge, with Heaven knows who walking past—"

"Quite," he concurred, with a finality that closed the subject.

They consulted their menus, and a waiter took their order. As they waited for the food to arrive, Jenny looked across at him: his skin was bronzed and leathery, from many years exposed to a foreign climate, and his jowls sagged, which was not unexpected for his fifty-odd years; but underneath it all she believed she could still see traces of the face she remembered. He was still very handsome, she decided.

"It's good to see you again," she said, "after a lifetime of correspondence."

"You were much better at writing than I was," he confessed.

"You wrote when you had to."

"That doesn't sound very friendly, does it."

"You've been the best of friends. I couldn't have asked for more."

He smiled at her, and their food arrived.

"So," she said, once they were alone again, "how are you finding living over here? Do you like England?"

"Oh, yes!" he said, tucking heartily into his rack of lamb. "Altogether more civilised."

"You don't miss your old life at all?"

"Not really," he said. "In many ways I think I'd outgrown it. And it's good to have fresh challenges. I was delighted when you asked me."

"Well, I'd kept up with your career, hadn't I? And I knew you from the first, practically."

"You did."

"And once I'd lost Rosalind—"

"Rosalind?"

"An old friend of the family."

"Ah."

"Once I'd lost her, well, you were my only connection with the past."

"I'm glad," he said, and wiped his moustache with his napkin.

She laid down her fork. "I find it so cold," she said.

"The omelette?" he asked, concerned.

"No, you scamp!" she said, amused. "I mean the weather! I miss the sun. I miss that intense heat."

"Even after all these years?" he asked.

"Even after all these years." She smiled and took another mouthful.

Once the plates had been cleared and they were alone with their coffee, she folded her napkin and said, "So, I really just want to thank you, to thank you so much, in person, for what you've done."

"Oh, Jenny," he said, almost shyly. "It was nothing."

"Hardly," said Jenny wryly. "I feel I owe you something."

"No. Really."

"That I should pay you."

"Absolutely not!" He was adamant. "You owe me nothing. Besides, it would be dangerous. The less that passes between us the better it will be for everyone. Even today is a risk. A considerable risk."

"I know," Jenny acknowledged. "Thank you."

"I've destroyed all your letters on the subject, and you've destroyed all mine, haven't you?"

"Yes, I have," she said.

"Haven't you?" he repeated with extra emphasis.

"Of course," she confirmed, slightly cowed by the strength of his insistence.

He smiled at her again. "You owe me nothing," he reiterated. "Nothing. Besides," he added, mischievously, "I enjoyed it."

"I believe you did," she said, and she looked him in the eyes, half in fear, half in admiration. "Oh, John," she said, "John Styles – my little Jackie. What a life you've had!"

And suddenly he was five years old again, playing on a veranda in Delhi, with his babysitter looking on. He shook his still surprisingly red hair, and beamed at her. "You play the best games, Jenny," he said.

2005

High Holborn

It was a dingy office, and the grey day outside made it feel even gloomier.

"Well, I think that's everything," said Mr Stevenson, the solicitor who was dealing with Jenny's affairs.

"Good, good," said Robert, sitting upright in front of the lawyer's desk.

"All the bequests are pretty much straightforward. We can realise all the stocks and shares and add them to the monetary assets. This will more than cover the specific bequests to the grandchildren and so forth, and still leave an acceptable sum over to divide between the four of you. The only slight complication is the house in Trowbridge."

"Yes, well, we've had a chat about that amongst ourselves."

"Ah, good. And?"

"Susan, Brenda and I are happy to leave it as it is, if that's okay. So Wendy can go on living there."

"That seems sensible. We could look into her buying the three of you out."

"Oh no, no. I don't think so," Robert protested mildly. "I'm sure there's no need for that."

"Very well. We could perhaps draw up some sort of agreement, just to keep everything cut and dried and above board."

"Well – if you think it's necessary."

"Might be an idea."

"Okay."

"I'll look into it."

"Thank you."

"Oh. And, er, there's one other thing," said the solicitor, searching through the papers on his desk. "There's this," he said, picking up a sealed envelope. "It's a letter from your mother addressed to you. Left with us to be delivered after her death." He held it out to Robert.

"Oh – er…" Robert faltered as he took it, slightly thrown by the sight of the familiar handwriting on the blue Basildon Bond envelope.

"I've no idea of the contents, of course, but you'll acquaint yourself with them soon enough, I'm sure. I'm always available if you need any advice." He stood up and held out his hand. "Thank you so much, Mr Markham. I'll be in touch."

"Yes. Thank you," said Robert, standing up also and shaking the solicitor's hand.

* * *

He took the Tube across London to Victoria Station, and once he was ensconced in an overground carriage all to himself he took his mother's letter out of his pocket. He and Maria had moved down to the coast some years ago, and the girls were almost grown up by now; well, Christine *was*, and Samantha wasn't far behind her.

It felt strange, seeing his mother's handwriting again, slightly shaky as it was in her latter years, though still regimental. He'd seen it often, of course – she was an enthusiastic letter-writer later on in life – but this was a communication from beyond the grave, as it were.

He tore across the top of the envelope and pulled out its contents just as the train jolted into motion: two sheets of blue Basildon Bond notepaper to match the envelope, all four sides covered in Jenny's clear ballpoint script, neatly set out in closely packed straight lines. It was dated the ninth of October two thousand and three, two years before her death.

"Dear Robert," it began, "I have something to tell you. Something I can't tell you face to face. While I'm still alive, I mean. While I'm still alive it will present you with a terrible dilemma, and I don't wish to make life difficult for you. I don't wish life to be difficult for any of my children, or grandchildren come to that – that's part of the point, really. After I'm gone, well, then it's up to you.

"I've just learned that a friend of mine, John Styles, has died, which is the reason I can write this letter now. He died quite peacefully from old age, I understand, though it's something of a surprise that I've outlived him. I used to babysit for his parents in India, you see. But he has no living relatives, so nothing I can say now will do any harm."

And then she went on to explain, clearly and fully, how she had set in train the events that led to Aidan's death, had contacted John Styles and furnished him with all the information necessary to carry out the murder. The letter shook slightly in Robert's hand as he read.

"Brenda's situation was impossible," she offered by way of explanation. "And Sharon's too. I couldn't let it go on. I had to do something. I'm sure you'll understand. And even if you don't, well, what's done is done, isn't it.

"My life used to be so exciting," Jenny wrote in conclusion, "but time and circumstances let me down terribly. I had hoped that you might pick up where I left off – and you did a little, I suppose – and I'm sure you're happy now – at least, you seem to be. Sharon will make her mark, I've no doubt of that. Already has, with her exhibition in London. I was so proud.

"But as for me, well, all I could do was to make my life a drama in itself. Which I did. You'll have to agree that I did, whatever stance you take on what I've just told you in this letter. And perhaps one day you'll tell the story, Robert – not to the police, I don't mean, though of course you can do that too if you feel you ought to – but to the world. I'd like that.

"There we are then. That's off my chest, though not off my conscience because it was never on it. I did the right thing, I know I did. For Brenda and Sharon. Many years ago I pretended to commit murder on stage – I did so, every day, for nearly three months – so it seems only fitting that I should have done it now for real – albeit at one remove.

"Thank you, darling. You've been a fine son to me,

whatever choices you may have made. I'll sign off now, and leave this letter with Mr Stevenson.

"Your loving mother,

"Jenny Markham née Pearson."

Robert looked out of the window as the train came to a halt at Rochester station. Doors banged and soon a middle-aged woman with a dog let herself into the carriage where he was sitting. They exchanged a friendly "good afternoon" and then she took a magazine from her bag and started to flick through it. Robert slipped the letter back into its envelope and put it away in his pocket.

This book is printed on paper from sustainable sources managed under the Forest Stewardship Council (FSC) scheme.

It has been printed in the UK to reduce transportation miles and their impact upon the environment.

For every new title that Matador publishes, we plant a tree to offset CO_2, partnering with the More Trees scheme.

For more about how Matador offsets its environmental impact, see www.troubador.co.uk/about/